"I HAVE OF COURSE HEARD OF YOU, MR. GUNSMITH...

Everybody has heard of you. Have you not heard of Carla Onterra, sir?"

Clint shook his head. "Sorry to say so, but I haven't."

"I show you something?"

"Depends what."

"You see that horseshoe on the post?" And before he had time to reply she had drawn the Colt at her right hip and fired. The young woman's gun was already back in its holster as she said, "You will find the hole dead center."

For a moment the Gunsmith said nothing. Then slowly he said, "I am sorry you did that, miss. That post didn't need a hole in it."

Don't miss any of the lusty, hard-riding action in the
Jove Western series, THE GUNSMITH

And coming next month:
THE GUNSMITH #68: FIVE CARD DEATH

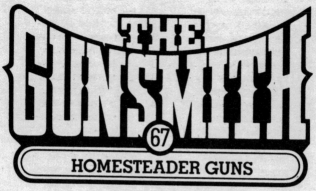

THE GUNSMITH

67

HOMESTEADER GUNS

J. R. ROBERTS

JOVE BOOKS, NEW YORK

THE GUNSMITH #67: HOMESTEADER GUNS

A Jove Book/published by arrangement with
the author

PRINTING HISTORY
Jove edition/July 1987

ISBN: 0-515-09058-1

Jove Books are published by The Berkley Publishing Group,
200 Madison Avenue, New York, New York 10016.
The name "JOVE" and the "J" logo
are trademarks belonging to Jove Publications, Inc.

PRINTED IN THE UNITED STATES OF AMERICA

10 9 8 7 6 5 4 3 2 1

ONE

Clint Adams' sense of humor was tickled as he stood looking at the new headboards in Kilton Wells' cemetery. And he remembered too how the Kilton Wells *Teller* had reported the droll affair at the Double Eagle Saloon. Clint had been watching the game, seen how the play had stripped down to a cattle dealer named Tom Silvers and a drummer named Al Pfouts, both professional gamblers, as were the others who had dropped out of the game.

The hand had brought real money to the table, and the pot grew larger until the final call. The boys had been drinking some, it should be added, by the time Silvers laid down a hand with three aces, and Pfouts one with two.

At this point a tall man named Bliss stepped in quickly as self-appointed referee to enforce the peace by ruling the pot should remain intact and a new hand dealt. To emphasize this decision he tore up the fifth ace. Tension mounted throughout the room as the men picked up their cards.

After the next draw, the raises and back raises came fast until once again only Pfouts and Silvers were active. And when the two hands were laid down, Silvers had two aces, but Pfouts, with a big grin, showed three.

This time there was no peacemaking. With his left hand Silvers drew the pot toward him, and with his right drew a gun and drilled Pfouts, who fell down beneath the table, bleeding profusely.

Clint refused to interfere, stepping back while the other players jumped in to claim a share of the pot. As they argued, Pfouts rose from beneath the table, his gun drawn, and shot Silvers, killing him. This deed accomplished, he slid back down to the floor. And gave up the ghost.

A coroner's jury was impaneled on the spot, and returned a swift verdict that the twin deaths had been due to "natural causes." After searching Pfouts' pockets the jury found another ace. Inside Silvers' shirt they found two more.

Clint had followed the whole affair, which only took some twenty-four hours to transpire. A day later, as he looked at the two headboards, he chuckled out loud at the three aces painted on Pfouts', and the two on Silvers'. But the best chuckle was that no one had even bothered about the names of the dead men.

Twenty minutes later he led Duke, his big black gelding, out of the livery barn and paid the old hostler for taking care of him.

"That there's a real handful of hoss you got there," the old-timer said.

The Gunsmith was pleased. "I see you took good care of him," he said.

The hostler bridled a bit at this. "I do my good job and I keep my nose clean," he said with spirit. "And by God, I know hossflesh when I see it."

Clint grinned as he handed the old man money. "I can see you do," he said.

The other man's eyes had dropped to Clint Adams' waist. "Got your rig out back," he said. "Nobody gave it any bother. Kept my eye on it close like you told me."

They had walked to the rear of the livery away from the street and now stood facing the team and wagon that was the Gunsmith's shop. Clint wrapped the reins of the big black horse around the wagon's endgate, not tying them firmly but just enough so Duke could feel the fastening, yet not so tight that if he jerked away from the wagon his reins would snap.

He ran the palm of his hand down the thick neck of the black horse. "All right, Duke boy, we're heading out. Just follow easy."

As he swung up into the wagon seat and picked up the lines of his team of bays, he caught the smile on the old hostler's face.

"You got a friend there," the old man said.

Clint nodded, settling into the wagon seat, and watched the hostler's eyes drop again to his waist.

"And I reckon another friend right there. You be the one they call the Gunsmith, I reckon."

Clint Adams felt again—for the thousandth time— the irritation sweep him as he heard the name that a newspaperman had pinned on him, loading him with the unwanted legend of ace gun mechanic. Some even claimed he was greater than his friend Bill Hickok, and whenever this particular bit came to his ears, Clint

Adams was filled with scorn.

Only now looking at the old hostler his annoyance abated as he saw that the man was not just repeating gossip or indulging in hero worship, but merely stating a fact. The remark clearly had been triggered by his admiration for Duke. And so the Gunsmith returned him his usual answer.

"That's what some people call me," he said.

"Name here is Tolliver," the hostler said. "Clay Tolliver."

Clint Adams nodded, suddenly hearing more in the other man's words than just the information. Did he know that name?

The hostler, who had been working on a pretty heavy chew of tobacco turned his head slightly, squinted up at the morning sky, and then let fly with a streak of tobacco juice at a pile of dried horse manure.

And it was just in the precise moment that he hit his target that he suddenly straightened, his mouth fell open, and Clint heard the crack of the rifle.

The Gunsmith was out of the wagon seat with his gun drawn before the hostler hit the ground. In the next breath he heard the horse pounding away down the main street in the early dawn. He knew it was useless—nor was it any of his business—to mount a pursuit.

Kneeling beside the body of the old-timer, he watched the blood darkening the hickory shirt and he felt something go out of him in the presence of this stranger's life so suddenly cut away. Clint Adams had seen many men die, and he had killed his share too, but this particular killing was somehow different. There had been something different about the old hostler. He had been touched by him.

He rose to his feet, holstering his Colt. There was

nothing to do. Only the usual. He turned and walked around the livery until he reached the street, which, save for three saddle horses outside the Clean Whistle Saloon, was deserted. Nothing unusual about a rifle shot first thing in the morning in the average western town, he realized. Nothing unusual about an old livery hostler getting shot, he told himself as he started down the street to see if he could locate the marshal.

TWO

The May morning had come gently to the Arizona desert, which was beginning to green, a sure sign that the bloom that comes in early summer was not far off.

The Gunsmith had driven his team and wagon up a long slope, in Big Tom Valley, and now drew rein, looking back at Duke who was tied to the endgate and had been following along at a leisurely pace.

"Good enough, big fella, we'll take a breather here." He had stopped by a small stand of trees and was fairly protected from anyone inquisitive enough to wonder what he was doing there. Settling his Stetson hat a bit forward on his head to give his eyes more shade, he lifted his canteen and took a drink of water.

He was looking down into a secluded basin at a four-room stone house and a corral, some outbuildings, and a barn. There was something almost idyllic about the scene, and he wondered how that could possibly fit into Buzz Fahnstock's character. His old friend had written him urgently, and so Clint hadn't hesitated, but had immediately closed up shop where he'd been working his gunsmithing trade and had come on out to Kilton Wells. As luck would have it, he hadn't been all that far away when the crumpled letter reached him.

And he'd debated whether or not to bring his rig with him, deciding that if there was trouble, as Buzz surely had indicated, then something like his gunsmith shop could serve to throw off the inquisitive; in short, it could be a good cover for him in getting around unnoticed. In short, he'd be seen as gunsmith and not gunhawk.

He thought now about his friend's letter. Buzz Fahnstock had always been a man to handle trouble, and had never asked for help before. But in his letter he had hinted strongly of dire and mysterious happenings at the homestead he'd taken after retiring as a lawman. And Clint Adams remembered with a grin that the name Buzz Fahnstock meant "one of the best, one of the toughest, one of the honest ones."

And suddenly he was thinking again of the old liveryman taking the bullet between his shoulder blades. A clean shot.

Right on target. Or had it been!

Had the old man really been the target? Or had that bullet really been intended for himself, for Clint Adams, the Gunsmith?

The town marshal, still sloppy with sleep and the odor of last night's booze, had no idea why anybody would want to shoot old Clay Tolliver in the back.

"Clay didn't carry no enemies that I ever heerd of," the marshal had said.

"Except one," the Gunsmith answered wryly. "It only takes one."

The marshal nodded slightly; he had a headache. "It only takes one," he echoed.

And the Gunsmith had left it at that. He'd done all he could. He had already called on the marshal the day before to identify himself, as he always did when entering a new town, just in case his reputation happened to get in the way of any trouble. Like now. But it was all right. The marshal, whose name was Abel Tymes, knew men that Clint knew; knew he could depend on the Gunsmith making no trouble. He was pleased now when Clint gave him money for the funeral.

"Never knew him, huh," Tymes observed, speaking a little close suddenly.

"He took good care of my horse, and my team and rig," Clint said with his eyes directly on the other man, who looked away.

"He'll be buried good," the marshal said, nodding twice to emphasize his good will.

Clint had it in his mind to ask Tymes if he knew Buzz Fahnstock, but something stopped him. He knew the marshal was thinking that whoever had killed Clay Tolliver might have been trying to get the Gunsmith; and yet Tymes had said nothing. For sure the marshal was playing it close to the vest, and Clint knew it was no time to expose his reasons for being in Kilton Wells.

Now, looking down at the house he took to be Buzz Fahnstock's, he remembered his friend telling him what the doctors had said: that his lungs were in bad shape and he might not have long to live. That was more than a year ago, and in the interim Clint had thought now and again of his friend; and indeed he'd been surprised to hear from him, thinking that he could maybe have been dead by now. But there was strength in Buzz's letter; the old boy was still very much alive. He hoped so. Clint hoped his friend was very much alive.

He had pulled his team and wagon further into the protection of the mesquite trees and now swiftly untied Duke from the endgate. He checked the saddle cinch, tightened it, talking to the big black gelding as he did so, for Duke was as much his friend and surely his companion as any person.

"We'll leave the team and take a ride on down for a look-see. I'm pretty sure that's got to be Buzz's place, from his description."

He had only just said those words when the sharp bark of a rifle and the ping of a bullet sounded as it struck a rock close to Duke's feet.

The Gunsmith was into the saddle almost before the big black horse could react. Swinging sharply over the ridge, he dropped down into a draw on the other side. Judging by the sound, he reckoned that the shot had come from two or three ridges over, probably from the top of a high, flat-topped rock.

Pulling up now, he dismounted and groundhitched Duke. Then, making his way carefully up the draw to a point where he was screened by mesquite trees, he walked a quarter of a mile, then crawled on his hands and knees until he could look down past the high flat rock onto the ridges beyond.

Lying under a spreading live oak tree, he detected movement a quarter of a mile away. Shading his eyes, he spotted a horse and rider moving slowly along the next ridge.

At first the rider was blurred by some scattered paloverde trees, but when finally the horse emerged with its rider from the brush into a clear space, Clint felt his breath catch.

The rider was a woman. He could see the stock of a rifle protruding from her saddle scabbard. Had she fired that shot? Why? Was it the same person who had perhaps fired at him at the livery and hit the hostler? Still in his surprise, Clint Adams watched until the woman disappeared over a ridge.

He waited, studying the distant ridge where the rider had disappeared, working his eyes slowly over the middle ground, the foreground, listening to the land all around him. Nothing. Only the life of the land and the sun burning down from the deep sky.

Clint had decided not to follow the woman; she was too far away for one thing, and, besides that, he could have been riding into a trap. And again, had she been shooting at him, the Gunsmith? Or had she mistaken him for someone else. Had it been merely a warning shot of some kind? This was cattle country, and Clint Adams was well aware of the feuds and outright wars that were a definite part of the life here in the Southwest.

There was nothing further to do here. He waited another moment, then mounted Duke and rode back to his wagon and team. It was getting close to noon as he drove down into the lonely basin with the firm-looking stone house and corral. Maybe there would be an answer down there, he was thinking. Maybe Buzz Fahnstock knew the answer; or at any rate, maybe his friend had the right question.

THREE

If he had expected his old friend Buzz Fahnstock to answer his knock, Clint Adams was in for a giant surprise. She didn't look like Buzz Fahnstock in the face, and as for the rest of her, Clint could feel his pulse pounding all the way down through to his suddenly rigid penis.

She was wearing fawn-colored riding breeches, the tightest pair of pants he'd ever seen in his life. She was facing him, and he knew without looking that her buttocks had to be just perfect. Those nipples pointing out from beneath the lemon-colored silk shirt proclaimed perfection, youth, eagerness in every inch of her. Her green eyes danced across his smiling face.

"I'm Clint Adams," he said, his eyes matching hers, while also fully aware of the thrust of her nipples as she stepped back from the door to let him enter.

"I know," she said simply. "Mr. Fahnstock is expecting you."

"Nice to be expected," he answered, grinning. "Uh—at least in the proper manner." And his eyes dropped to her breasts which were barely restrained by the silk lemon-colored blouse.

"And I'm Wendy Quinn. I live just a ways up-country. I've been helping Buzz—uh, Mr. Fahnstock, whenever I can."

"I can see he can't be wanting for anything then," Clint said pleasantly. Then, realizing that she might take his remark in a more personal way, he said quickly, "I mean, I feel happy to see he has such an efficient person handling things for him."

She had colored slightly at his words, but not in anger, rather in simple embarrassment, obviously feeling the power of his glance as his eyes felt fondly over the lemon blouse.

"Where is the old buzzard?"

"Come." And she led the way to another door, knocked, and when a gruff voice said, "It ain't locked," walked in.

The owner of that gruff voice was lying on top of a buffalo robe that was spread over a bed at the far end of the room.

"Clint! You got my letter!"

"I sure did. And me and Duke got here as quick as we could."

"Still got the big black, have you?"

Clint, fully aware of the girl Wendy, even though she was out of his line of vision, now heard the door shut behind him.

"Where did you get that cute helper, you old buzzard?" he asked with a grin as he pulled up a chair and sat beside the bed.

The man on the bed chuckled. "She lives on the next ranch, north of here, the Box T. I knew her father—till he got shot dead by the sons of bitches who're trying to push all of us out of the country; or into it," he added sourly.

"So you couldn't just settle down easy like and take care of your health," Clint said. "I told you, you'd never retire. You live a life like we do, Buzz; and it'll follow you everywhere."

"That by God is what I am finding out."

Buzz Fahnstock was a big, stocky man in his late forties, or maybe early fifties, and but for the lung trouble he was having, had always been strong as a Brahma bull. A man to ride the river with, Clint Adams was thinking.

The man on the bed was fully clothed, but resting. "Doc says I got to go slow for a spell," he explained, watching his younger friend. "I've had this damn thing on and off. A lot of the time I feel pretty good, but then suddenly without any warning—wham! And I'm flat on my back again."

Clint Adams was a young man still, in his early thirties, about six feet, plus maybe an inch in height, slim and strong, with no extra flesh. Buzz Fahnstock knew his strong point. Those fantastic reflexes that made him the fastest gun, more than likely of them all. Buzz also knew that his friend was somewhat bitter over the fact that the major part of his reputation lay in his ability with a gun. He'd been a lawman, as had Fahnstock, but he was known now as a fast gun. And Buzz Fahnstock knew that what Clint had just told him about retiring was true. At a certain point, using a gun had to become living by the gun. It had been that way with him until he'd gotten to be a lunger, and it was that way with Clint Adams.

There came a knock at the door then. It was Wendy with two mugs of steaming coffee.

The Gunsmith commented again on how lucky Buzz Fahnstock was to have such a handy helper.

"I better tell you, Clint." Fahnstock had lifted himself up onto an elbow. "I better tell you the sawbones says I got the consumption. I don't let that get around, you understand."

"Does the girl know?"

"You and her are the only ones. Her dad knew, till the bastards . . ." But he was suddenly overtaken by a wracking cough.

"Why don't you just give me the story," Clint suggested. "And then take it easy. Give me the main stuff; I can figure out the details."

The man on the bed lay back, wheezing. "I'm glad you're here, Clint," he said finally, getting the words out with some difficulty.

"Take your time, Buzz. We've both got all the time we need."

It brought a grin to his friend's stubbled face. Now, while Buzz collected himself, Clint told him about Clay Tolliver's shooting, and the woman who might have taken a shot at him from the ridge. Fahnstock had no idea why anyone would want to shoot the old hostler, and much less of a notion who the woman with the rifle might be, or why she would take a shot at Clint Adams.

"'Course it could have been a warning shot, figuring you to be a squatter," Fahnstock said. "It's what the big stockmen figure folks like us to be."

Buzz's story was simple, and Clint knew most of it already. But he was looking for a clue to the woman with the rifle, and so he was eager to hear what his friend had to say.

Buzz Fahnstock, journeying around the West after spending most of his life in the Montana and Wyoming territory, had finally settled in Arizona, hoping the dry air would prolong his life.

The man who had been one of the toughest lawmen in Wyoming and Montana homesteaded three hundred twenty acres of land southwest of Tucson, within the shadows of the Sierrita Mountains. With the help of a few Mexicans he built his rock house and corral, dug a deep well, and made other improvements.

Buzz Fahnstock told his friend Clint that he'd hoped to acquire additional acreage for pasture and go into the cattle business, for it was ideal cattle country. His decision had been motivated too by the sudden death of his wife Ellie. And so, with characteristic vigor, yet tempered by his illness, Buzz had started to build his outfit.

"Excepting others had the same notion," he told Clint wryly. "A lot of 'em seized the best range and been trying to freeze out all the squatters, as they call us."

The Gunsmith nodded his head ruefully, familiar with the old story. "And the fact that those fellers had been homesteaders themselves not so many years before doesn't make any difference toward you and the other newcomers," he observed.

"Not a damn bit," Buzz said, sitting up now and bringing his feet around to the floor. "They aim to either buy out the homesteaders' land at a cheap price, or force them through intimidation to abandon it. I'm saying that real polite," he added sardonically.

Clint Adams knew well enough that the wealthy cattlemen would not fight Buzz Fahnstock in the open, for that wasn't the way they sought to discourage squatters. Their campaigns concentrated on destruction and intimidation and were usually carried out by hired riders from outside the area.

Buzz Fahnstock was on his feet now, and as far as Clint could tell was in pretty good condition, though he realized that his friend could suddenly be overtaken with weakness. Still, he remained seated while Fahnstock left the room, calling out to Wendy for more coffee.

He was back shortly with the mugs, and, sitting on the edge of the bed, went on with his story.

Once he decided to fight for his homestead—and Clint knew that for a man like Buzz there couldn't have been any other decision—the ex-lawman went about the country trying to organize other recent settlers so that concerted action could be taken against any person who might try to exert pressure against them. To his surprise, Buzz quickly found that instead of being willing to cooperate with him, most of the homesteaders were already discouraged and were willing to sell.

"Damn piss-poor few of them had sand enough to fight for their land. Clint, I'm telling you it's a sad thing to see what some men will put up with. I ended up with too damn few to make any kind of effective organization."

"So you decided to go it alone." Clint Adams had pushed his chair back so that he could tilt a little as he looked at his friend.

"You would have done the same, by God."

"I reckon." And his grin was warm.

"Then I thought of buying up some land," Buzz said after taking a pull at his coffee. "Figured if them others could gobble up land, why couldn't I do the same thing."

"Didn't know you had that kind of money, Buzz," said the Gunsmith, adding, "'Course, that is your business."

"I don't, but I got a rich brother back in Illinois, and I made some contacts when I was doing better than I am now. It was a possibility, Clint. So I got some money together and had a try at it."

"What happened?"

The man sitting on the edge of the bed sniffed, nodded his head reflectively and said, "I picked up five holdings. Came to 1,280 acres; excepting none of it adjoined my own land. They were scattered about in a twenty-mile radius. There was one homestead bordering me on the south which I tried to buy and which would have given me access to two others I'd gotten hold of, but the owner—feller named Marsh Cantwell—held out for more than I wanted to pay. See, the others came cheap, I mean reasonable, being as the people were ready to sell to the big cattlemen anyways." He took another drink of coffee. "So that's where I'm at now. I have heard the tale that Cole Diamond is bringing in some special guns now."

"Cole Diamond?"

"He's the head of the cattlemen."

"And what's he?" the Gunsmith asked.

"He's a sweetheart."

His friend's sour tone was all Clint needed to get the picture of Cole Diamond's character.

A silence suddenly fell between the two men now, and Clint noticed how his friend was watching him.

"Clint, can you stick around a while?"

"Why not?"

"I can't get about like I used to; I could use a extra hand. A good hand. See, I figure Diamond was back of John Quinn's killing. 'Course I can't prove it. Wendy feels the same."

The Gunsmith knew how much it cost Buzz Fahnstock to admit his inability to get around as he had formerly. Yet there was no bitterness in the man's tone, no self-pity.

"I've got my rig with me," Clint said. "I don't see why I can't pick up a little money here and there working over a few guns. There's bound to be customers about, wouldn't you say? And I'm looking forward to getting into some work. Man gets rusty if he doesn't keep at it."

Buzz Fahnstock was grinning. "You can have the whole of the bunkhouse there," he said. "Wendy'll help you get spread out if needed."

The Gunsmith nodded to his friend in appreciation as in his mind's eye he saw again the trim, yet fully formed figure of the dark-haired Wendy in the tight, fawn-colored riding pants. And he was doubly delighted when, after taking care of his team and wagon and feeding Duke, he carried his warbag into the bunkhouse and found the girl making up his bunk.

"I've got bedding right here," he said, dropping his bag to the floor.

She was bent across the bunk, tucking in a side, and spoke to him over her shoulder. "Suit yourself, but I think you'll be comfortable with this."

Clint tore his eyes away from her buttocks as she straightened and turned to face him.

"I think I'll be just fine," he said.

"Is something the matter?" she asked suddenly.

"Buzz says you live nearby," he said, avoiding an answer, and wanting to keep her in conversation with him.

"Not far." She nodded her head, her eyes alight as she looked directly at him. "North."

He could feel his excitement growing; even her voice stirred him. But he didn't want to rush things. He knew she liked him. He knew she was feeling what he was feeling. He knew there was time; they could take their time.

FOUR

To the Gunsmith's delight the expression of his full desire came much sooner than he had expected. He had just gotten into his bunk that very evening, following a long session of reminiscence and projected planning with Buzz Fahnstock, when he heard the knock at the bunkhouse door.

He was alert instantly, his hand reaching to his Colt, thumbing back the hammer, raising his head slightly the better to hear.

Another knock, a little louder, and it was followed by a voice calling "Clint Adams!" In a moment he was out of bed and standing in the middle of the room, yet out of any firing line from the door.

"Mr. Adams. Clint Adams!" The voice was a loud whisper.

Clint stepped to the side of the door, and opened it. She entered silently.

"I wanted to . . ."

"I know," he said simply, holstering his gun. "So did I."

He closed the door, bolted it, and watched her walk to a chair and sit down. There was something, a shyness he decided, in her movement. It was as though she'd had to make a difficult decision to come. He didn't take that to mean that there was a question about her wanting him, but rather that the girl wasn't so sure of herself that she would just assume that he would want her.

"I like you, Wendy," he said, sitting down in the chair opposite her. "But I want you to come only if you're sure, clear."

Her green eyes were shining as she let them move over his face earnestly. And then suddenly she seemed to relax all over and a smile filled her face.

Clint felt something draw him to his feet as it did the girl; almost like a string connected to the two of them. And then they were standing there with their arms around each other. He felt his member pushing into her as her legs parted. He had slipped his hands down to feel over her buttocks, while she slipped her arms around his neck and, with her legs wider apart, now received his organ through his bursting trousers.

He moved his hands to the front of her breeches and began undressing her as she reached down and ran her palm on the tip of his mounded trousers. He felt his passion bursting and now she melted more and began unbuttoning him.

In seconds they were naked with her straddling his rigid cock, squeezing it with her thighs, while he cupped one breast with his hand, feeling its spring, the erection of its large nipple with delight. With his other hand he roamed down her back to feel the crack between her deliciously firm buttocks.

She was murmuring in his ear as he brought her down onto the bunk, her legs falling apart while she drew up her knees and he played the tip of his erection into her wet clitoris. Now she reached down to fondle his balls, tickling her hand into the place just between his legs behind his scrotum, then slipping up along his great shaft to guide him to her soaking vagina.

Clint was quivering with delight at her combination of knowledgeable sexuality and innocence.

Now he raised himself slightly as he drove his organ deep and high into her while she gasped with utter delight, her buttocks moving with his slow rhythm. Gradually he increased as she began to gasp more, even now all but saying words of exquisite joy as he stroked her faster and faster and she opened deeper and deeper, until they were soaking, with her come wet on his thighs. Faster they rode each other as she clutched his pumping buttocks until in the final burst of ecstasy they came together, and came . . . and came . . .

FIVE

The next morning Clint saddled Duke and rode into Kilton Wells. He had no plan in mind, but thought he would simply browse around town and see what he might pick up on local gossip.

Halfway through the afternoon he had covered all three saloons, the barber shop and bath, the local eatery, and the building known as the Metropole, which passed for the town hotel. He'd picked up a good bit of local news and gossip, though nothing much that he thought would be of any use. But it was while he was having a beer in the Double Eagle Saloon and Gaming Establishment that the idea came to him to go see Marsh Cantwell whose homestead bordered Buzz's on the south, but whose price had been too high. But first he wanted to check Buzz. He rode out of Kilton Wells in the later afternoon as quietly as he'd ridden in that morning.

He had ridden around a low butte and out into a

clearing surrounded by paloverde trees when suddenly a horse bearing an empty saddle broke through some brush at the side of the trail and galloped off into the desert.

"What do you reckon that is, old fella?" he asked Duke, who had let go a low nicker as the other horse appeared.

Clint kicked the big black gelding out of the trail and followed a line of tracks to the other side of the bushes.

He was almost on top of the woman before he saw her. Duke spooked out of the way just in time, for she'd been partially hidden by the bush near which she was lying.

He took a quick look around to make sure it wasn't some sort of trap, then dismounted, groundhitching Duke. Squatting beside the woman, he felt her pulse. Her lids fluttered suddenly and a pair of puzzled hazel eyes looked up at him.

"What happened?" he asked.

She gazed steadily at him for some moments before replying, as though attempting to sort out her thoughts. "I—I don't know. I guess my horse must have thrown me," she said at last. "Something scared him, I believe. Something in the brush."

The Gunsmith bent closer to her to examine a swelling on her temple. "Looks like you might have hit a rock when you fell. Except there's no blood. Sure that horse of yours didn't throw his head and knock you out?"

"I expect he could have," she conceded. "I don't have a martingale on him and he does toss his head a good bit." She sat up and felt the lump on her head. "Whatever it was it must have been a pretty hard blow, because I was knocked unconscious."

"I'm mighty sorry," Clint said, his voice expressing real concern. He waited a moment, taking in her good looks. She must have been about twenty-five, a tall, well-formed girl with long blond hair, widely spaced hazel eyes, and a high bosom that looked absolutely inviting. "I'll see if I can catch your horse," he said.

Quickly, he mounted Duke, and after about twenty minutes managed to catch the estranged animal after cornering it in a clump of mesquite.

When he noticed the rifle stock protruding from the saddle scabbard, his eyes tightened with quick interest. He drew it partially out, enough so he could tell its caliber.

Then he led the horse back to the girl and watched her mount. She was even taller than he had thought, and she was wearing loose trousers, though they were by no means baggy, and did absolutely nothing to hide the delightful curves of her buttocks and thighs.

He could tell she was by no means a poor rider as she swung her horse around—a chunky little blue roan with two white-stocking legs.

She smiled down at him pleasantly. "Thank you so much for helping me. It was very kind of you."

Without another word she rode off, leaving him with a vision of rather distant-looking eyes that now seemed more brown than hazel, the impression of a lithe, fully sensuous body, and the teasing trace of an English accent. As he watched her gallop down the trail, he belatedly realized that he had neglected to ask her name. But he decided not to follow. Somehow he knew he would meet up with her again.

Puzzled, he headed toward Buzz Fahnstock and his TeaKettle ranch, the TK brand now showing up on some of the livestock he was passing. He had no way of being sure but he thought the girl was the woman he had seen on the ridge, the one he had thought might have taken the shot at him. Yes, he decided, she had to be English, or at the least, an easterner.

When he told Buzz Fahnstock about the little drama along the trail, his friend was more curious than alarmed. Indeed, Buzz was more concerned with some news that Wendy had brought him, that his closest neighbor, Noah McAdoo, had strung a barbed wire fence along his west line.

"If I run any cattle on the two homesteads I bought west of me, it figures I'll have to drive them clear around McAdoo's spread. The damn fool is cutting me off and making my new holdings useless to me. Like this they'll not be worth a damn cent."

Clint thought a minute on that and then asked to see Fahnstock's map, which he had drawn carefully for him the day before.

After studying the map for only a moment Clint nodded, handing the paper back to Buzz, who was seated at his table in his bedroom. "I just wanted to check."

"Check what? The size of the hole I'm in?" Buzz ran his long fingers through his hair.

"Your other neighbor Marsh Cantwell."

"He won't meet my price. I told you, Clint. I offered him fifteen-hundred dollars, but he wants twice that. It isn't worth it."

The Gunsmith was shaking his head. "Buzz, I think it could be worth it in the end. You'd have protection, and access. McAdoo's got you jammed both ways from the middle."

They argued it back and forth until finally Fahnstock agreed that three thousand dollars might be all right, especially as it would give him access to his other holdings.

"I'll ride over and see about it tomorrow," he told Clint. "Might make a deal if he's in the right mood."

"Make it," Clint said with a grin. "It's the only way."

Later that evening, when the knock came at the bunkhouse door, he realized how eagerly he'd been awaiting her.

There was still a trace of shyness with her, but it hardly lasted the moments it took for them to undress each other. Each knew what was in store this time, and it was almost impossible to go slowly.

He was inside her even before she lay down, slipping his huge erection up into her eager wet slit as she moaned and melted against him, standing on one leg with her other raised so that he could enter more easily, and swiftly. Then, holding him around the neck, she lifted her other leg, coming right off the floor to sit on his organ, wiggling herself to receive it deeper and more joyfully as he could hardly stand, still moving his hips to pump her as he bore her to the bed. And still pumping together they came in a massive criterion of delight.

They lay supine on the bunk, his fingers laced in hers as, side by side, they looked up at the dark ceiling of the cabin.

"Clint, you're the most wonderful lover," she said softly, speaking her words toward the high roof.

"It takes two, Wendy. Neither one nor the other partner is responsible for the joy, or the lack of it, either," he added. "So I can only say that you are wonderful too."

"It's you who make me wonderful then," she said with a small laugh, turning toward him and snuggling into his neck, like a little girl in a sudden attack of shyness.

And already she had her leg across his body, her hand coming down to brush his stirring member. She ran her fingertips along its growing length, then, as it hardened, she took it in her fist, rubbing its head against her leg.

Now he reached down and began playing with her already soaking slit, teasing his fingers into her lips, sinking one finger deep into her and wiggling it.

All at once she had moved down and had her lips on the head of his cock, kissing it with little pecks as he thought he would go out of his mind. Her tongue came out and she began to lick its head, now licking down its wet shaft, and finally, when he thought he would go raving mad, she slid its great rigid thickness into her mouth, and deep, all the full length to its hilt. Clint thought she would choke but somehow she had either learned or had born in her an expertise that handled his size superbly, although when she released him as he withdrew, a gurgle came from her and she started to cough, but he was already mounting her, sliding deep and high again as she opened with her legs as wide as they would go and as high. He brought them up onto his shoulders as he raised up to drive deeper into her, so that she was almost on the back of her neck.

She was gasping for breath, muttering, begging. He didn't know what, for he could hardly hear anything himself, such was the fantastic quivering that showered his body as again he let her legs down, riding her gently now as he felt her belly warm against his, her lips on his mouth, kissing and begging for all that he could give her.

"More, Clint, more. Dear Clint, come, come,

come!" She cried the words, biting his cheek, his ear, his neck, her buttocks thrashing as she reached the climax with him, and he thrusting as far as he could go, and more, and finally touching the end of her as he rubbed the head of his cock against her inmost wall and came in a perfectly timed explosion with her.

He lay limp and satiated in her arms, spread on top of her without a muscle in his body moving, or a thought. Finally he rolled off her and they both lay there side by side. For a while they slept.

It was close to dawn when he awakened. She had stirred beside him and now, without a word, their hands felt each other and it seemed not very long before they began once more to discover each other's bodies. This time they took longer. The need was just as strong, but softer, gentler, and for Clint and the girl too—more satisfying.

When she left him she was glowing with happiness and he was singing inside his body. He knew it was going to be a good day.

SIX

In the morning Buzz Fahnstock's cough had come back and seemed to be worse. It turned out he'd been up with it a good part of the night, and now he looked haggard and obviously was extremely tired.

Wendy insisted that he stay in bed, telling him he needed rest, and appealing to Clint.

Clint didn't have to be persuaded as he saw his friend's drawn face, heard his wracking cough.

"Let me go talk to Cantwell," he said. "I'll tell him I'm just acting on your behalf."

"Clint, I don't want any of them to get wind that I'm laid up. If they do they'll be in on me like an avalanche."

"Don't worry. They'll hear nothing from me," Clint promised.

"Nor me," echoed Wendy. "Now you lie down. Please!"

It was about the middle of the forenoon when the

Gunsmith rode over to the adjoining ranch. No one was in sight as Duke came down the draw that brought them to the buildings and corrals at an angle. But Clint did take note of Marsh Cantwell's dun gelding standing in the round horse corral without any rigging on him. The animal looked gaunt.

Clint took a careful look around before swinging down from Duke and wrapping his reins around the hitch rack in front of the main building.

He knocked on the door, but there was no sound from inside. He knocked again, louder this time. And then a third time. Again he took a look around at the buildings and corrals. Nobody in sight. Only the dun horse. Curious, he pulled the latch string on the door. And finding the door unlocked he pushed it open.

The shock of the sight that met his eyes was quick and done with immediately. He'd seen plenty of dead men, and he hardly noticed his reaction as he narrowed his eyes on the man lying on his back in the middle of the floor, his arms outflung. The swarm of flies buzzing around him told that death had occurred some time before, possibly three or four days.

It had to be Marsh Cantwell; the Gunsmith just knew it was with that extra sense that came to him so often in moments of crisis and quick and violent action.

What had happened was quite clear. Cantwell had been killed by a bullet that had struck him squarely in the back.

When he went outside the cabin, Clint took time to carry some oats to the half-starved dun horse. He watched him eating, not allowing him too much, then led him to the watering trough outside the barn. Finally, he led him into the barn and tied him in a stall. He spent some time examining the dun, checking his feet, going

over his whole body carefully. The animal had gone a
good while without water or feed. He had the urge to
give him a rubdown with some twigs he found on a pile
in a corner of the barn, but didn't want to take the time
right then. It was necessary to get into town and report
on Cantwell's death, and then tell Buzz what had happened. Clearly, the stakes were reaching the limit.

When he walked out of the barn he saw the three
riders. They were quartering down the long draw and as
they hit the flat land coming into the ranch they broke
into a brisk canter. At first he wondered if it was Marshal Abel Tymes and deputies, but quickly saw it
wasn't. They were riding in as though they meant business; as though they knew something. He had that sudden flash that this was no casual dropping by.

He didn't have to look at the sky to know it was
reaching noon. The hot disk of the sun was burning
right down into his Stetson hat. He knew they could see
him now as he quickly, yet without any obvious hurry,
changed his position so that he would not be facing the
sun when the three rode in. Rather, the light would be in
their eyes. He let his hand brush the Colt at his side,
was aware of the .22 caliber Colt New Line in his belt
inside his shirt—his belly gun. He wondered if they
recognized him now as he saw it wasn't Tymes but two
stringy gunhawks flanking a big man wearing a Mexican straw hat with its broad brim curled native fashion,
held by a buckskin thong tied beneath his big chin. A
big man, not Mexican, looking to be in his early forties,
squat, lumpy-faced with deep-set gimlet eyes shaded by
black, bushy eyebrows. Despite the heat, he wore over-
alls tucked into high-heeled western boots, and a brown
woolen shirt. From the description Buzz Fahnstock had
given him, Clint knew this had to be Cole Diamond,

leader of the cattlemen who were determined to wipe out the squatters. His companions needed no names. Clint had never seen either of them before, but he knew the type like he knew the back of his hand.

And he knew what they were going to do. They were already doing it; the pair of gunhawks starting to spread wide of Diamond, the better to triangle the lone man standing by the barn.

"I think you can hold it right there!" The Gunsmith's words were soft but nonetheless penetrating. They were quiet words, insisting on being heard.

And it was interesting to see the hard surprise that came into Cole Diamond's face, the anger that hit the two hawks.

Diamond was the first to recover, raising his hand as he drew on his reins. "Reckon you really are the Gunsmith!" he snapped out with a hard grin, shoving his jaw forward. "Kind of touchy, ain't you." His companions had pulled up their horses making little clouds of dust.

"No hard feelings," the big man went on, while the man on his left spat over his horse's withers. The man on his right leaned on his saddle horn and sniffed. They were very much themselves again. Back with the business they'd evidently brought.

"I'm Cole Diamond," the man with the big Mexican hat said. "I'm here on business with Marsh Cantwell. He about?"

"He is inside." Not for a minute had the Gunsmith taken his eyes off the three men.

"Then if you don't mind we'll dismount and I'll get to my business with him."

Clint Adams nodded and Diamond swung down from his big sorrel.

"I'm offering you a job, Gunsmith. Name your figure." Cole Diamond's voice was sour as he stood facing the man who had stopped their momentum so abruptly.

"I don't hire my gun, Mr. Diamond," Clint replied easily.

"You've been out at Fahnstock's place so I know you're working for the squatters. I'll double what they pay you, triple it."

"Sorry, Diamond. I'm not working for anybody. Buzz Fahnstock happens to be an old friend of mine. I just dropped by to visit him a spell."

The big man had wrapped the sorrel's reins around the hitching post not far from Duke and now he started toward the house.

"You say Cantwell's inside?"

"As the saying goes, he has taken up permanent residence."

Hearing this, Diamond's thick lips pursed. He glanced toward his two gunmen, then glanced back at Clint.

"Cantwell's dead," he said, as though to make sure.

"Go and take a look."

A low whistle escaped the big man's pursed lips. "Maybe I'll just take your word for it. I've heard how fast you are with a gun."

"I didn't kill him. He was shot in the back with a rifle."

Diamond's big eyebrows lifted at that. "Who did it then?"

"I have no notion," Clint said sincerely. "But he's been dead I'd say two, three days."

"It must've been more than two days ago," Diamond said swiftly. "I saw Marsh on Friday. Said he was plan-

ning to pull out and asked me to drop by before. This is
my property now, by the way. I bought it from Cantwell
last Friday."

"Do you always ride with gunmen, Diamond?" Clint
asked.

The big man held his arms out from his sides. "I am
not armed." There was a defiant smile on his face as he
spoke.

"I'll be riding in to tell Marshal Tymes," Clint said.
"I guess he'll send men out."

"I'll be glad to help in any way I can," Diamond
said, more agreeably as he saw the way things were
going. "You're figuring it's better for Tymes to see him
out here, better than packing the body into town? My
men could help."

"No, we'll leave him, Tymes will want to look for
clues. And he'll want to know about Cantwell's homestead."

"What about his homestead?" Diamond came back
fast. "I bought it from him last Friday. It's my property
you're standing on."

"You have a bill of sale, have you?"

He watched the big man's eyes narrow. Diamond
reached into his pocket and pulled out a rumpled piece
of paper and held it up so that Clint could see it, but
Diamond was holding on to it firmly. "You note the date
on it," he said. "That shows Cantwell was alive on Friday. Not that I have to tell you in the first place," he
added. "But you can look so you can tell Fahnstock and
his friends."

The paper was a crudely written quitclaim deed to
Cantwell's homestead, stating that this deed was being
given in "consideration for one dollar and other consid-
erations." It was dated the previous Friday.

The Gunsmith studied the paper for a moment and then watched Cole Diamond fold it and put it back in his pocket. "So how much did he sell for?"

A tight smile hit the corners of Diamond's eyes then. "Don't know as that's any of your business, is it?"

The Gunsmith had fallen silent, quickly thinking it through. "Tell you what we'd better do," he said suddenly. "That money might still be on him. If it isn't, then whoever killed him robbed him. Let's go in and take a look. I didn't touch a thing."

For a moment Clint thought Diamond was going to refuse, but he must have seen there was no getting out of it. He shrugged, and nodded.

In Cantwell's pockets the only valuables they found were two crumpled ten-dollar bills, four silver dollars, and some smaller coins.

"The body doesn't look as if he was robbed," Clint said. "Nobody went through his pockets. Let's search the premises."

Diamond nodded. "I'd like to send my men back to the ranch. They're not doing any good out here. You got any objection?"

"Go ahead."

An hour later they closed the door of Marsh Cantwell's cabin and mounted their horses. They had found none of the money Diamond claimed to have paid Cantwell.

"He sure got it all right," Diamond said. "Al Wales, one of my hands, and my foreman Tiny Hinds witnessed the transaction."

"Why didn't they witness the quitclaim deed he gave you?" Clint asked pointedly.

"Don't need any witnesses for a quitclaim deed. All

you need is the signature for the party giving it. The Land Office has that signature on file."

All of which Clint Adams already knew, but he wanted to hear what Diamond would say. They rode in silence until in about half an hour they came to a junction of two trails.

"My outfit's yonder," Diamond said, reining the sorrel. "I guess you know Kilton Wells is that way."

Clint nodded. "I'll be giving the whole story to the marshal."

"I'd like you to remember, Adams, that when you tell Tymes about this be sure to mention I have two witnesses to that transaction. I don't want any false notions to get around."

"I reckon you can handle that little bit of information yourself, Diamond. I reckon you're going to have to," he added under his breath as he kicked Duke into a brisk canter.

He was thinking how interesting it was that Cole Diamond had known who he was.

SEVEN

Clint debated whether to pay a quick visit to Buzz and tell him what had happened or to ride into Kilton Wells and get Marshal Abel Tymes. Riding directly into town from Cantwell's place would have made a quicker trip than going by Fahnstock's TeaKettle Ranch. All the same, he decided to get the news to Buzz right away. Something was giving him the feeling that whoever had killed Marsh Cantwell might shortly step up the attack and maybe try to bushwhack Buzz; and, besides, he was concerned about his friend's health.

To his astonishment he found Buzz not in bed where he had left him but out by the barn taking a loose shoe off a big rangy bay horse. Buzz looked as good as Clint had ever seen him, with his sleeves rolled up and his big shoulders bursting at the seams of his denim shirt as he held the bay's left hind leg in his lap, standing in a half squatting position while he filed and buffed the hoof. To be sure, he was coughing every now and again, and strongly, but this didn't appear to deter him at all.

"Glad to see you're following doctor's orders and doing all you can to rest and recuperate," Clint said wryly.

Buzz grinned, wiping the sweat from his forehead with the back of his forearm. "Man's got to keep active, Clint. If he don't he'll just dry up. Hell, you know that better than me." And at that moment the cough hit him, doubling him over until at last he straightened up, red-faced, gasping, trying to grin, like a little boy caught out.

"Where is Wendy? Not within a mile of here I'll be bound, or she'd be riding herd on you."

"Reckon she would have been here if she knew you were about, my friend." And the look on Buzz Fahnstock's face was doleful as he started to cough again.

The Gunsmith caught it immediately. "I do believe you have notions about that young lady."

"A lot of good that does me." Fahnstock was in good humor and Clint was glad he was. He'd had the brief thought that Wendy might have been his friend's private property, but when he'd asked her if he was trespassing in any way she'd scouted the idea, telling him she liked Buzz a lot, but—period. He was glad to see that he hadn't stirred any hard feelings.

"You know I'm not the possessive type, Buzz."

"I know that, Clint. And I appreciate your saying it."

Buzz Fahnstock put his hand on the bay's leg. "Reckon I'll have to put a set of shoes on him," he said. "But he'll have to wait. I ain't that healthy yet. I see you've got news."

"You'd better lie down."

"I hate to have to agree with that."

When they were inside the house and Buzz was on his bed, Clint related what he'd found out at Marsh Cantwell's outfit, plus the details of his encounter with Cole Diamond and his brace of gunswifts.

Fahnstock smiled when he got to the part with the two gunnies. Then his face tightened. "They'll carry that back with them, tell the others. Clint, the whole damn bunch will be gunning for you."

"Plus the mysterious lady."

Buzz nodded sagely. "Plus the mystery lady."

Reaching into his shirt pocket Clint brought out a fired rifle cartridge and held it up for his friend to see. "That's the one that kicked up the dirt at my feet the day I got here," he said. "I took a sashay over by the place just for another look; and there it was."

Fahnstock took the cartridge and examined it. "A .44," he said softly. "Plenty of guns around here that this would fit," he went on. "By the way, what kind of a gun was that girl carrying in her scabbard—the one that got dumped from her horse?"

Clint nodded. "It was a .44. But I must say she sure didn't look like the type of young lady who'd be going around trying to bushwhack young fellers like myself."

"Maybe she has ambition to be Number One Gun of the West." Buzz Fahnstock's look was wry and pointed as he regarded his friend. And then he squinted. "Tom Finger come by while you were off. He tells me Cole Diamond hired more guns."

"You and me could take a ride over to Cantwell's when you're better and when I get back from seeing Tymes. I might have missed something and you knew him."

"Why after you see Tymes? We can ride over in the morning."

"Think you'll be up to it?"

"Would you like a punch in the nose?"

"Just asking."

"The doc told me to take it easy. He didn't tell me to climb into my coffin."

And when Clint said nothing he went on. "I'll take my little buckskin; hasn't been ridden in some while." Then he added, "No funning, I'll be better in the morning. And I want to see the place before Tymes tears everything apart looking for that money."

The next morning, true to his prediction, Buzz Fahnstock was chipper as ever, and after an early breakfast they took the trail to Marsh Cantwell's place.

Clint couldn't get away from the feeling that the whole situation in which he found himself in regard to his friend Buzz was just too loose, too vague. At least except for the killing of Marsh Cantwell. There wasn't any doubt that it was murder plain and simple. And certainly there wasn't any vagueness about Cole Diamond and his gunmen; he wholly believed the picture that Buzz Fahnstock presented him with. But the woman who he was pretty sure had taken a shot at him; who was she? And if it was not she who had fired that .44, who had? And why? And was she the same as the girl who had been thrown from her horse? Neither Buzz nor Wendy had any notion who the woman or women might be. And then, what about the hostler? Had that bullet been intended for him, for the Gunsmith? Or was the killing, the bushwhacking of Clay Tolliver quite separate from the cattle trouble? Somehow, the Gunsmith thought not. He had the distinct feeling that the shooting of the old hostler was indeed connected with the efforts of Cole Diamond and his fellow cattlemen to get the new homesteaders off their land.

As they rode into Cantwell's spread, Clint quickly noted that the dun horse was still there.

"It appears nobody's been about," he observed to Buzz who, he was happy to see, had taken the ride well.

But the Gunsmith's pleasure at his friend's condition was turned to shock when they opened the door of Cantwell's cabin and entered.

The body had disappeared!

They spent the rest of the day searching for it, and the money, but found nothing. By nightfall they agreed to give up. Yet they were not totally empty-handed. Clint had found tracks of three horses leading north, with one of the horses obviously carrying something other than a rider. A dead man? But they decided not to follow when the tracks became less visible in the desert.

"I'd better get in to report it to Tymes," Clint said as they decided to bed down in Cantwell's cabin for the night. "It seems to me things are getting hot, and we don't want to spend all our shots on one target."

"I'm with you on that," Buzz said, as he lay down on the one bunk offered by the Cantwell cabin. He was wheezing again, and now and then coughing.

From the floor Clint said, "You better head straight back from here in the morning, Buzz. While I'll head for town."

But his friend didn't hear him. All the sound that could be heard was a loud, rolling snore from the bunk.

In the dark the Gunsmith smiled to himself. He was pleased at the sound of that snore. It came from a man who was going to have a good sleep.

EIGHT

Marshal Abel Tymes tilted back in his chair and spat with hard accuracy at the battered spittoon by the leg of his desk. "Hell," he said. "Not even a body to bury."

"Nothing to bury, nothing to mourn." The Gunsmith was seated on an empty, up-ended crate just a few feet away from the marshal of Kilton Wells. He was studying the other man, knowing that something was working its way to the surface. Tymes was a sardonic man, stolid, and a defender of the law, though not a foolhardy one. He had always tempered his sense of right and wrong with sober judgment in regard to his own survival. A man not without courage, the Gunsmith had heard, but he was surely going on seventy now and he had survived. This alone was no small thing.

A sigh rolled down Abel Tymes' long, bony nose, and down through his lean body. "Men like you, Adams; trouble seems never far behind."

"I know that, Marshal. And whose fault do you think that is?"

"When I was younger, like about your age, I used to wonder on that. But I figured finally it wasn't my fault. Not all of it anyways. Mostly it was those damn fools who want to build a man up so's they can knock him over."

"The newspapers back East pinned the label on me," Clint said, speaking without rancor, but with simple honesty.

"That's what I know," Tymes agreed. "'Course with myself I never got it in the newspapers and all that; and I am mighty glad. Only I had the reputation word of mouth if you know what I mean."

The Gunsmith nodded. "I do."

"Hell, no man wants to get himself shot up so some jerky damn fool can sing a big brag on it. But people want it. If they ain't building this one up they're building on that one."

The marshal leaned forward, dropping the front legs of his chair to the floor. "Well..." Lifting his Stetson hat up off his head by the crown, he set it down again, and rose to his feet, a knee cracking and his breath whistling from his tight lips against the sudden spasm. "Reckon I better get to work, Adams." He paused, straightening and looking the Gunsmith right in the eye. "Can I count on you?"

"I'm a friend of Buzz Fahnstock, like you know," Clint said earnestly. "So I've already taken sides."

"That's what I know. But I am still askin'. Deputies come scarce around this country. But I am not asking you to start wearing tin."

"If it's understood about Buzz."

A rueful smile came into the marshal's eyes, and his

lips thinned. "Wish sometimes I was in a place where I could take sides," he said softly.

Clint nodded, rising swiftly to his feet. "I know what you mean. I have been there too."

That afternoon Clint took the train to Phoenix where he visited the Land Office. He had learned from Tymes that Diamond would have filed his quitclaim deed there. The deed was on file and it meant that Cole Diamond was in full possession of the Cantwell homestead and Buzz Fahnstock was cut off from his holdings to the south.

Buzz received the news laconically when Clint related it to him on his return to the TeaKettle homestead. Then he offered news of his own. "I've had news while you were away. It appears Diamond is telling that I killed Cantwell for the money Diamond was supposed to have paid him for his homestead."

"Let me offer you some unsolicited advice, my friend." The Gunsmith eased himself into a chair to face the man lying on the bed. "Don't let on you know about it. Go about your business, just like you always do, and like you never heard anything about Diamond's story."

Buzz Fahnstock was already nodding in agreement. "I know."

"If you argue with them or challenge Diamond and any of the others on it they'll use it as an excuse to get you for good."

Buzz broke into a sudden laugh. "I hope you don't think those buggers think they need an excuse."

"No, not an excuse, but they've still got the semblance of the law—and even more I'd say after talking to the marshal—to deal with."

"Tymes?"

"That old boy has still got his guts," the Gunsmith said. "And they know it. They won't want him going to Phoenix to whistle up help."

Buzz Fahnstock took out a cigar stub that he'd been carrying in his shirt pocket for some time. Its odor was still strong, Clint noted, but shaking his head regretfully, Buzz slipped it back into his pocket. "Damn! Almost forgot I'm not supposed to smoke."

"I don't believe Abel figures he can get help out of Phoenix," Clint said. "He knows the big cattlemen have got everybody of any account on their side. Still . . ."

"Still, it's got to look good. I got 'cha," Buzz agreed.

"Of course, up to a point. We will not sleep on it," Clint said.

Buzz gave a rich chuckle at that. "That we won't. And it's good to know Tymes still has his balls."

Later, long after Buzz Fahnstock had gone to bed, and Clint Adams had received his nightly visitor, Wendy, once again insatiable in her need, commented on the subject of balls.

"I would like you to know, Mr. Adams, that you have the most lovable pair of balls that anyone could possibly hope for," she said as she snuggled up close to him after they had partaken of their delightful pleasure.

"I might say that you have a pretty damn fine pair of breasts, young lady."

She laughed into his chest as he slipped his arm around her.

It was a moonlit night and they were in the field behind the ranch, lying on a buffalo blanket she had brought for the occasion. The sky was scattered with stars, each one distinct from any other. And the smell of the land was rich.

"I'm so glad we came outdoors," Wendy said. "As a matter of fact, I think Buzz is beginning to think that we have something going together."

"Do we mind?" Clint asked mildly.

"No. Not really. Only I wouldn't want to hurt him. I'm very fond of Buzz."

"He's very fond of you," Clint said.

"I know. That's why I wouldn't want to hurt him."

"Right. He's a good man."

"I like you, Clint."

"And I like you, Wendy."

She lifted her weight a little and raised up on an elbow, looking down at him. "I understand," she said simply. "But I still want you—like this."

And she reached down to take his stiffening organ in her fist and started playing with him. He was hard instantly and his whole shaft was wet as she stroked him. Leaning down she sucked him and licked him, and tickled him all over his crotch with her tongue, teasing him to an almost unbearable delight. Then she climbed on top of him and sat down on his great stick, wiggling her hips and looking down at him. He reached up and took each breast in his hands. They were firm, almost too big for his hands, but he managed. They were exquisitely shaped, turning upward toward their hard pink nipples, and when he released them they sprang with their marvelous resiliency. He took one in his mouth. And when he released the nipple from his sucking she pushed the other to his lips.

"Don't play favorites, for God's sake!" And she groaned with joy as he sucked and chewed gently on each of her teats in turn.

Finally he pushed her gently up and slipped almost out of her, stopping just at the tip of her clitoris.

"Oh no, oh my God, no!" she begged. "Don't take him out!"

But he had no intention of removing his organ of delight. He plunged into her and, gripping her buttocks, rolled her over onto her back and then rode her beautifully to a delirium of exploding joy.

NINE

Only a couple of days later the Gunsmith and Buzz Fahnstock were riding toward the latter's homestead after checking neighbor McAdoo's barbed wire fencing.

It was a summer night, with heat lightning flashing across the desert. Coyotes could be heard howling and the land seemed charged with some sort of expectancy. Clint figured a storm was coming. He was about to comment on this to his companion when suddenly they both heard the dry drumbeat of hooves, and all at once a horse broke into the trail ahead of them, running hard. But neither of them could distinguish anything special about the rider.

"Who the hell can that be?" Buzz speculated. "Pretty late for anyone to be out."

As they rode, the hoofbeats gradually died away.

"Whoever it is he's in some big hurry," Clint said.

At that moment Duke suddenly arched his neck,

snorted, and sashayed sideways to the edge of the trail.

"What is it, big fella?" Clint asked, reining the black horse. He swung down and Buzz followed suit. Both men cautiously approached the spot where Duke had shied.

"There's something there all right," Buzz said. "Looks to be something round."

Clint had picked up a rock and tossed it, but got no reaction. "I think it's a hat," he said.

It was. Buzz took the hat from him to examine it with a lighted lucifer.

"Looks like a woman's hat," Clint said. "See those little holes in the crown? That's where a hatpin went through."

Fahnstock whistled softly between his teeth. "What do you figure a woman's doing out here in the night, off the trail. Waiting for us?"

"I don't know. But she was in too big a hurry to come back for her hat when it dropped off. He shoved the hat down between himself and the pommel of his saddle as they rode off. He was wondering who the woman was. Was it the woman who had shot at him? Was it the woman he'd met after she'd been thrown by her horse? Whoever she was—or whoever they were, if they were two—was a mystery that seemed set on remaining a mystery.

As they rode toward the Fahnstock homestead a chill came into the night, though Clint felt it as a pleasant change. He was no longer thinking about the woman but was back to figuring how to help his friend Buzz keep his land. For the two of them to go up against an army of gunmen that Cole Diamond obviously had at his command was sheer stupidity, not to mention suicide. What alternatives offered themselves besides such a rash act? As far as he could tell, so much obviously hinged on Diamond. Buzz Fahnstock and Wendy kept asserting this. Cole Diamond was not a man you could easily replace. He was a man with an iron will and hand and he was utterly without scruple. The Gunsmith had seen that in his face and bearing, and he had heard it around Kilton Wells and from Buzz Fahnstock and Wendy Quinn. But the Gunsmith wasn't about to murder anybody. He killed only in self-defense or in a shoot-out.

As they climbed the ascending trail of the last ridge before the TeaKettle, a light became clearly visible coming from the top of the ridge, a light shooting through the sky.

"By God, it looks like a fire," Buzz observed.

The Gunsmith kicked big Duke into a run to the top; for there was a fear clutching to him. And his fear was surely founded, he immediately discovered.

"It's your place!" he yelled back at Fahnstock. "They've set fire to it. Come on!"

Together they pounded down the long draw to the homestead, urging their horses, who needed no urging, especially Duke, but urging them nonetheless with their will, their fear for what damage had been done, and even the fear that possibly Wendy Quinn might have been there and gotten caught.

In minutes they came pounding up to the edge of the blaze on lathered mounts, with Buzz on his buckskin a good bit in the rear of big Duke. They were just in time to see the roof of the barn fall in. Both leaped from their horses and began tearing at the corral which was already ablaze. The heat was tremendous and they had to keep going back, driven by the scorching flames and smoke.

It seemed an interminable battle, but finally they

managed to save most of the other buildings including the main house and bunk house, and most of the corral. However, the main fire had spread to dry grass and this they battled for a good hour before bringing it under control.

For a while the two of them had been too busy for speaking beyond the barest communications, but finally they were able to turn toward the house. Buzz suddenly stopped and stood stock-still staring in through a smashed window. For a moment Clint thought he was going to fall, his face was flushed, his breathing was labored from the incredible exertion they had both just undergone.

Inside the house was some burned brush. Evidently it had been lighted and pushed through the broken window, only the dry leaves had burned so quickly that the danger had passed before Clint and Buzz got there, for neither one of them had seen any fire in the house. The flames had swept up to the stucco ceiling but hadn't done much damage, only blackening a part of one wall. And the flagstone floor was intact.

"Whoever did it," Clint said, "was in a big hurry. He didn't wait long enough to see if the house would catch."

Buzz had lighted a lantern and was studying the scorched wall. "You mean, she didn't wait, don't you?"

"The girl, huh? You figure the girl, the woman, did it."

"There are two of us—right? So she must have decided it wasn't the moment to shoot you, or maybe me for all I know. And so she galloped ahead and fired my place."

"You really think she did it?"

For a moment Fahnstock was silent and then he said,

"Damned if I know. It just seemed likely." And he started to cough. He was clearly exhausted.

Clint went outside the house to where he had hitched Duke and found the hat which he had shoved into a saddlebag. When he came back into the house he sniffed it, then held it for Buzz. There was unquestionably a faint aroma of perfume coming from the hat.

"That's for sure a woman's hat," Clint said. "But that doesn't mean she fired your place."

When they finally went to bed it was very late. Clint lay awake for a while thinking about the fire and the strange woman and wondering where Wendy might be. He hoped she was safely back home. And he thought too that he'd better be seeing her soon. His body agreed. There was no question about that he told himself with an inner grin just before he slept.

His sleep was not deep. As always when in a tense situation, Clint slept close to the surface, only half asleep as it were; and during the night he awakened with his hands on his six-gun. Not a deep sleep, but a safe one.

The next morning they were both up early, with Buzz Fahnstock grimly looking over the damage to his property and Clint checking for sign of who the fire-setter could have been.

His findings were meager, but then he was at last rewarded.

"Do you use matches like this?" he asked Fahnstock, handing him a small paper box that he'd found in the brush in back of the house.

Buzz carefully examined the box which had Searchlight Matches printed in red on two sides. At one end the cover had been torn open in the shape of the letter V.

"No," Buzz replied. "Where'd you find them?"

"Back of the house. Do you ever open matchboxes like that?"

"Never have. Never seen anyone else who has either."

The Gunsmith slipped the box into his pocket. "Well, all right, but somebody around here does. And I figure that somebody was the one who set fire to your barn last night and tried to burn down your house."

Buzz Fahnstock's eyes seemed to Clint to turn inward as though some thought had occurred to him. But the moment passed quickly as they both heard the sound of a horse's hooves coming in swiftly.

"One rider," said the Gunsmith. And Buzz nodded.

It was Wendy, and they saw she'd been pushing her little pinto horse. She all but jumped out of her saddle as the pinto came to an abrupt halt and ran toward them as though she was about to embrace them both. But she stopped short, slightly out of breath, and, Clint noted, with her marvelous breasts heaving, the nipples hard as they pushed against her checked cotton shirt.

"Where have you both been? I've been so worried!" And suddenly she saw the ruined barn, the scars on the house. "I smelled something. Yes, charred wood, burned. My God, what happened?" Suddenly her eyes opened wide. "And you, what are you doing? Trying to kill yourself? Is that it!" "And you! You let him!"

Clint was speechless and at the same time touched by her concern.

Under her onslaught poor Buzz took a step backward. "Wendy..."

"You get right to bed!"

They were both pleased at her concern, at the way

she chivied them—half mother, half little girl—demanding to know what had happened.

"If you'll build us a cup of coffee we might tell you," Buzz said with a soft, weary smile. He was truly exhausted.

Wendy didn't wait, but led them into the house and began to get coffee. For more than an hour they sat together drinking the coffee and talking over the possibilities of who it might have been who had set the fire, placing it within the context of the bigger fight with the cattlemen. What to do? How to defend themselves and keep their land?

"Are you all right up there on your outfit?" Clint asked the girl. He looked over at Buzz. "Maybe she ought to move down here for a while, Buzz. What do you think?"

"I think that's a good idea. I've Clancy Calhoun coming over to help keep an eye on things when one of us isn't around."

"Good idea."

Wendy had her eyes on Clint. "I appreciate it. I'd love to. But please be sure you want me . . ." And he watched how she tore her eyes away from him to direct the rest of her sentence to Buzz.

"Consider it done," Buzz said. "You'd better get whatever you need and bring it down. We'll of course still keep an eye on your place, but Clint's right, there is no sense in you staying up there alone. It'd just be asking for trouble."

Wendy could barely disguise her pleasure as she got up and started to the door. Nor could Clint Adams keep his eyes from her superb rump as she crossed the room. When the door closed behind her he found Buzz looking at him with a smile.

"I'm glad you still appreciate the finer things in life, Clint."

"Glad you do, Buzz."

They fell silent then, nursing their coffee cups. At last Buzz said, "Hard to see this thing through, I mean apart from a more-sooner-than-later gunfight. All I can say is I'm ready."

"One thing we can do is take a look at that quitclaim deed again. I mean, to check it for forgery." Clint said. "I had no way of checking that when I found out the claim was actually filed. I didn't know Cantwell's signature."

"I know it has to be forged," Buzz said, coming down hard on the words. "Cantwell would never have handed over his outfit like that. Never! He was a tough bugger, but he was straight in his way. And I know he was holding out. He didn't want to join up with me, but he sure didn't want to roll over for Diamond. He told me he was doubling his price to Diamond." He coughed. "I know they murdered Cantwell. He was a tough one, but he insisted on going it alone, maybe if he'd joined with me he'd still be alive." He coughed again, bringing up spittle. "Or maybe I'd be dead with him."

TEN

The Gunsmith had long ago discovered that one of the best ways to think things through was to be working at something that occupied his attention while at the same time with an inner, or deeper, attention he would silently work at the problem that was confronting him. One of his best ways of thus occupying the surface of his thoughts while his deeper thoughts were engaged elsewhere was with his gunsmithing.

Clint loved working over guns, repairing, cleaning, improving, trying out new ways of making a gun more accurate, easier to handle in shooting and also in drawing it from its holster. Balance, timing, the perfect locking and unlocking of its parts were essentials that he felt could always be bettered.

On this particular morning as he was working at his wagon "gun shop," he was surprised and pleased suddenly to discover that he had an audience—as well as an interested pupil. Especially pleased because the person in question happened to be Wendy Quinn.

While he continued working on a Colt single-action that a customer in Chipping Rock had left him and had never returned for, the girl plied him with questions about what he was actually doing, and about gunfighting. Clint didn't like questions about gunfighting, but he certainly liked Wendy and so he modified his reactions to some of her questions so as not to be too short with her. After all, he had discovered, she had been sent to school in the East and therefore wasn't as aware of many of the western "necessaries" that some other girl brought up locally would have been. Likely she wouldn't understand his aversion to his own reputation.

"It's called slip-hammering," he explained in answer to her question on what he was doing with the Colt. "This is a single-action Colt, meaning it requires two actions to fire it. First the cocking with the thumb, and then squeezing the trigger finger." He held the gun up to illustrate it as the noon sun burned down on them, baking the hardpan ground of Buzz Fahnstock's yard. "See, in the double-action, the same pressure that squeezes the trigger also turns the cylinder one chamber, raises the hammer, and releases it. You get double action for the same effort, and faster, more accurate shooting."

"But that's a single-action," she said brightly, leaning forward and snatching his attention to her thrusting breasts so that he almost made a mistake in removing the trigger of the gun. Yet he recovered, smiling inwardly at himself. "See here, you either remove the trigger like I'm doing, or you tie it back, and you draw the hammer back to full cock with your thumb. Then to fire it, you just slip your thumb off the hammer." He held up the unloaded gun and illustrated. "You save a few seconds, and that can mean your life, but you do lose accuracy. The double-action's a better gun."

"That's what I think too," Wendy said, her green eyes large, round, and shining as she held them right on his face. "But isn't it better to wear two guns?" she asked. "I notice you only wear one."

"Back in the old days before the war some men used to pack three, four guns, plus a few knives for good measure. Quantrill, you've heard of him?"

"Who hasn't!"

"Bloody William and his men mostly wore from two to six Navy Colts each, not to mention a few derringers and Bowie knives to feel a bit more secure."

"Isn't that overdoing it?" she said with a little laugh.

"In those days guns were hard to load and risky to shoot. It was sensible, 'course providing you were in that kind of a business."

He had raised the gun he was working on and was squinting along its barrel to see how it sighted.

"Before that time, before the war," he went on, lowering the gun and then picking up an oily rag to wipe it, "all the ammunition was at best a loose collection of ball, powder, cap, and a prayer that everything would go off as you planned it. There were some variations, howsomever," he continued with a slight grin. "Ball and powder were packaged together in paper sacks, or the bullet would be wrapped in buckskin to give it a tighter fit in the gun barrel, or there'd been some mechanisms invented by God knows who—to eliminate the ramrod, which took time. The only thing was the new mechanisms were complicated and subject to rust and failure;

whereas the old ramrod with no moving parts had been just about foolproof."

"So how did that get solved?" Wendy asked, leaning against the wagon wheel as one of horses in the repaired corral snorted suddenly and kicked at a fly.

"The metal cartridge did it." He put down the gun, wrapped in the cloth, and squinted at the sun, figuring the time of day.

"That's what you have now?"

He nodded, admiring the wisp of dark brown hair that was just touching her forehead. "The cap and powder were enclosed in a brass cylinder, and with the bullet crimped in a waterproof seal at the working end there was no longer any danger of an overcharge of powder, no longer the chance of powder getting damp with rain or even dew or fog." He spread his hands apart with palms up. "Simple, once it was figured out."

They were silent as he rummaged through a drawer in his wagon.

"You like working with guns, don't you?" she said.

"Better than shooting them."

"Is that why they call you the Gunsmith, I suppose," she went on, saying it not as a question but as a tentative statement, as though she wasn't quite sure.

"Let's say that's what I am," Clint said gently. "I'm a gunsmith. I fix guns, I rebuild them. But some people when they say 'Gunsmith' they mean something else."

"I see . . ." Her voice was soft and he liked the way she was looking at him.

"The thing is, Wendy, that simple animal cunning kills more men in this country than all other violent causes combined; including snake-bite."

He laughed at the sudden surprise in her face.

"Fact is, a shot in the back delivered at short range when the victim can't see the killer is highly effective. No question."

And suddenly he wished he hadn't said it. It reminded him in a searing flash of his friend Wild Bill. He hadn't been there in Deadwood, but the news had reached him fast. Bill, probably the fastest ever. Only it hadn't helped him when he sat with his back to the door and Jack McCall pulled the trigger.

"What's the matter?" Wendy said quickly, aware of the change in him.

"Nothing. Just thought of something. C'mon," he said. "I want to give Duke a rubdown. I mean—if you've got nothing you want to do."

"There's only one thing I really want to do," Wendy said.

He stepped down from the wagon and stood facing her. "Wendy, that is just what I want to do too."

"Well...?" Her lips were slightly parted and her breath had quickened. There was a flush of color in her cheeks.

Clint felt his own passion rising to total rigidity and had to clamp down on himself. "But we're going to have to wait."

"You mean on account of Buzz...?"

"No. On account of that rider who's coming in by that clump of mesquite just behind you," Clint said.

She turned to look. "What an inconvenient time for a person to come calling."

"I certainly agree with you, but perhaps you'd better go and see how Buzz is. He was taking a snooze a while back and I'm not so sure that our visitor ought to bother him. Of course, it could be it's for me."

The girl had started toward the house, now she stopped and turned toward Clint. "It could be trouble for you then, Clint. I'll warn Buzz. We can keep our eye on the man. I guess he's alone."

"Maybe alone," the Gunsmith said with his eyes on the nearing figure. "Yes, it could be trouble. Only it isn't a he; it's a she."

ELEVEN

She was not alone. Clint had spotted the two out-riders flanking her at a good distance, yet within rifle range. Now they were moving in as she got closer to the ranch.

He didn't like it. Not at all. Was she the woman who had shot at him? There was no way of knowing, since he'd not been able to get a close look that day. But that fact certainly didn't rule her out. She could easily be one and the same.

He had climbed back into his wagon, and after checking the Colt at his hip, he pretended to work on one of the many guns he was carrying in his shop. Yet although apparently attending to the work he had at hand, he was also fully aware of the approaching rider and escort. He was aware too that there could be more riders who were keeping out of sight.

As the woman got closer he saw she was riding a

big dappled gray. And she was handling him well. No
question about it, she cut a fine figure whoever she
was. He liked to see a woman who knew how to
handle her horse. Especially, of course, if she was
also good-looking. And to his searching eyes, the oncoming rider seemed to fill the bill. He saw long dark
hair flowing behind her as she now kicked her mount
into a canter, after reaching the bottom of the long
draw that swept into the flat and open space leading
directly to Buzz Fahnstock's TeaKettle Ranch. It was
a good approach, for whoever was in the house or
about the outfit could easily see oncoming riders.

Now, as the woman came closer she held up her left
hand, evidently signaling, and Clint saw the brace of
riders who had been accompanying her draw rein. He
still wasn't sure if she was the woman who had shot at
him, but now he could certainly see her good looks. She
was flushed as she cantered into the yard and pulled up
before him. Her cheeks, framed by masses of black hair
which swept freely behind her, were almost rosy. She
had amber-colored eyes which turned up at the corners
giving her a feline look while her mouth was wide, the
lips full; the kind that could easily pout or carry hard
words, cutting words. She was looking right at him as
she drew rein. And for Clint Adams the one word that
seemed best to describe her was "passion."

Clearly this was a young woman who could love and
hate with equal ease, equal intensity, and, he was sure,
equal frequency. She must have been no more than
thirty. He had instantly spotted the twin pistols she was
wearing in a buscadero, the wide, form-fitting Mexican
gun belt that also carried extra ammunition.

He heard one of his team nicker from the corral that
had escaped the fire as the dappled gray stopped, toss-

ing its big head and stomping once with its right fore-
foot. The girl was sitting in the tooled Mexican saddle
with the silver conchas as though she was growing
there.

Clint meanwhile had not put down the gun he was
pretending to be working on. He was seated on a low
pile of blankets and a buffalo robe in his wagon box and
now looked up casually at his visitor.

He knew that he was supposed to have seen the two
outriders, and so now he glanced meaningfully toward
the house, and again toward one of the remaining outbuildings, making sure the visitor understood that he
had men covering him. It was a maneuver he had de-
vised with Buzz, for they had expected unwanted visitors.

For a moment the girl sat on her horse and Clint
simply looked at her, not offering a greeting but waiting
to see what she had to say. The two outriders had re-
moved the need for western hospitality as far as he was
concerned. And he wanted her to know it.

"Are you the Mister Gunsmith?" The words came out
neutral, though with a Spanish accent, while the expression on her face was absolutely calm. It said nothing,
although Clint did feel that there was something like a
twinge in the first look she turned on him close up. He
had to admit he felt the same. She was so damn good-
looking.

"My name is Clint Adams," he said calmly. "Do you
have business for me?" And he hefted the Colt he was
working on just a little so that she was sure to know
what he meant.

"I am Carla Onterra, mister. I have heard you are a
good gunsmith, first grade, and I bring you this." And
as she spoke she drew the sidearm from her left holster

and held it up for him to see. It was a Navy Colt. Moving her horse closer to where he sat in the wagon, she handed it to him.

"I want it sliphammer, and I want the balance check for perfect," she said.

Clint was already caught by her interesting command of English, her appearance, and basically herself. Clearly, she was totally self-possessed. He didn't let his observations take him, however. He had already noted that she wasn't carrying a rifle on her saddle; though that didn't eliminate the possibility of her having taken a shot at him.

"When do you want it," he said, examining the gun.

"As soon as you have done it. I am expecting best work."

"I never give any less than that," the Gunsmith said. "That's a nice weapon you've got there. I see you've taken good care of it."

A cool smile touched the corners of her mouth. A moment passed with her expression not changing as she sized him up. Clint, for his part, was admiring the tightness of her thighs as they filled the red riding breeches that looked as though they'd been painted on her. He had detected too, and quite thoroughly without being overt, how she filled the turquoise-colored silk blouse with breasts that could only be thoroughly provocative.

"I have of course heard of you, Mr. Gunsmith. Everybody has heard of you."

Clint said nothing. He sat in the wagon casually at ease, yet totally alert, his eyes including the ground behind her, ready for the horsemen should they appear.

"Have you not heard of Carla Onterra, sir?"

Clint shook his head. "Sorry to say so, but I haven't." And he watched the streak of disappointment come into her face, followed by annoyance. Suddenly she was smiling.

"I show you something?"

"Depends what."

Her smile broadened into fun. "You see that horseshoe on the post?" And before he had time to reply she had drawn the Colt at her right hip and fired.

The horses that comprised the Gunsmith's team whickered loudly, then returned to kicking at flies.

The young woman's gun was already back in its holster as she said, "You will find the hole dead center."

For a moment the Gunsmith said nothing. Then slowly he said, "I am sorry you did that, miss. That post didn't need a hole in it." And he hefted the Navy Colt that she handed him for repair and tossed it to her.

She caught it with her left hand. Slowly she returned it to its holster. "I am sorry you don't want to play with me, Mr. Gunsmith. I suppose you could make a shot like that with no trouble at all."

"I wouldn't know," Clint said easily, his voice calm, though he could feel his irritation rising. Yet it was mixed with other feelings as he saw her breasts pushing angrily against her silk blouse. "You see, I don't play with guns. I don't ever draw my gun except when I have to." He touched his forefinger to the brim of his hat then. "Nice meeting you."

She lifted the reins of the dappled gray. "We will meet again, Mr.—Adams." With a low whistle at the gray horse she turned him and spurred at the same time.

Clint watched her all the way to the start of the long draw where she was met by her two flanking riders. All three ran their horses up the draw. He was still hearing how her Spanish accent had changed when she hadn't gotten what she'd wanted.

Before the riders were out of sight Wendy and Buzz had joined their friend. All three watched without saying a word. It was Clint who broke the silence.

"You know her?"

"Never laid eyes on her," Buzz said. "But she's an eyeful for sure." And he cut his glance toward Wendy, who made a face at him. "But she's not the type for staying long with a man I'd say. You got any notion who she might be, Wendy?"

"A mystery woman," Wendy said with an exaggerated sigh.

Clint grinned. He liked her sense of humor.

"What do you think, Clint?"

"I think I don't like people who run their horses uphill unnecessarily. She might know guns and she can ride but she sure doesn't care much for horseflesh."

Later, over coffee in Buzz Fahnstock's kitchen, the two men returned to the need for someone to go to the Land Office at Phoenix to check Cole Diamond's quit-claim deed for possible forgery.

"I'm in mind for a trip to Phoenix," Buzz said.

But his two companions turned on him like one person.

"No!" Wendy said, and Clint echoed her.

"But I'm feeling fine," Buzz insisted.

"You are staying right here," Wendy told him. And when Buzz turned appealing eyes to his friend Clint she even raised her voice. "Don't think you can appeal to him!"

Both men burst out laughing at that.

"But I need Clint here," Buzz said. "He can't go."

"I will go," Wendy said with a finality in her tone that seemed to settle the matter.

The two men looked at each other and grinned.

After a moment Buzz said, "Ten will get you twenty the signature on that quitclaim is a forgery."

"I won't fade you on that," Clint said. "But I will go to Phoenix, and I'm going to need something with Marsh Cantwell's signature on it, so I can make a comparison." He looked at Wendy. "You'd be too much of a target, Miss Quinn," he said gently.

At which Wendy stuck her tongue out and made a face.

TWELVE

In the back room of the Double Eagle Saloon Cole Diamond was just dismissing a half dozen of his men. He had previously met with the five cattlemen who, along with himself, comprised the Kilton Wells Stockgrowers Protective Association, of which he was the head. A decision had been arrived at unanimously, and not only due to the spur of Cole Diamond. The five saw the need, read the handwriting on the wall. Let one homesteader in and the squatters would be thick as flies in the summertime. No question. But, as Cole had pointed out, Fahnstock had the Gunsmith, and now it was necessary, imperative, to equal it. Cole Diamond said he had the answer. "John File," he'd said, laying the name down on the table final as a fourth ace.

"You figure File can take the Gunsmith, do you," said Lije Millerby.

"John File is about the fastest there is," Diamond had

replied confidently. "He buried the Choctaw Kid real quick. I saw it myself, like quickern' a cat licking his own ass. I say we hire him."

"I go with that," said George Macklin.

And heads nodded around the table.

But Lije Millerby said, "You've got a half dozen guns already, Cole. How come they haven't been able to handle it? I mean, six against one."

A toothy smile suddenly appeared in Cole Diamond's big face. It was one of his useful assets, disarming the opposition, though it didn't have that effect on Lije Millerby at the moment. "Lije, no matter how good a gunhawk might be, only a damn fool goes up against a man he knows... I say, he *knows* is better. You should've seen those two damn fools I had with me the other day when Adams backwatered them!"

"But six. But you've six of them!"

"It's true," Macklin said, coming in to stave off a possible dispute. "Let's go along with it, Lije. If those boys are scared of Adams, then they won't be worth a potful of cold piss if they were a dozen."

Lije had to grin at that. "Good enough. Just wanted to check it," he said. "Hell, boys, we don't want a range war on our hands."

They had all agreed with that, but all knew privately that if they couldn't win any other way then war it would be. Clearly John File was a step in the right direction. John File, everyone knew, was swift as silk; and it was clearly understood that he would be backed by the six.

It was only shortly after his colleagues had departed that Cole Diamond had held a meeting with his six "extra hands," explaining to them that John File had agreed to join the Stockgrowers Association as "a range detective." Cole had, needless to say, not mentioned to his fellow stockmen that he had already contacted File, who had agreed to take care of the Gunsmith.

And so, as he shut the door of his "Town Office" behind the last of his hired gunmen, he felt things were finally moving, things were going to work out. And with that concern off his mind, his thoughts swiftly turned to more pleasant subjects, such as relaxation and fun.

As if by magic, as though someone somewhere had read his thoughts, the door suddenly opened and the object of his thoughts entered the room.

"My dear! I was just thinking of you!" Cole Diamond's small eyes, which nevertheless saw a great deal beneath those black bushy eyebrows, opened wide now with eagerness as he looked at the dark-haired girl in the tight red riding breeches and turquoise silk blouse.

But in the instant that he said those words of greeting, Cole Diamond saw the flash in those amber-colored eyes and felt himself tighten all over.

"My dear, come in, come in. I'll get us a little something. What would you like?" And his smile came quickly, though not easily to his face. Cole Diamond knew a lot of things, and one of the most important things he knew was that he was madly in love with this unbelievably beautiful girl. He was a realist, Diamond, and he knew he was a fool for her, but he didn't care. He didn't give a damn. Still, his head cautioned him again and again to take it slowly, not to give himself up completely, not to make a fool of himself and do anything he would regret. And, in actual fact, he had been able to draw the line when it came right down to push or shove. He had refused her once or twice—for her demands were often outrageous. Once she'd even wanted a half interest in his saloon, the Double Eagle, which not everybody knew he actually owned. And another time she'd wanted his big sorrel stallion. It had been exceedingly hard to support his decisions in those two instances, for Cole Diamond was a man of insatiable and special sexual appetites, and Carla knew beautifully how to satisfy his cravings.

Other times he had given in, giving her a prize yearling and a favorite dog. And every now and again the grim realization came to him that she had him—to use his own words—by the balls. He was thinking this now as he stepped back to allow her entry to his private back room at the Double Eagle.

"I have heard that this man Fly, Jack Fly, will come to here," she said, her words cold as pieces of ice.

"File," Diamond corrected. "John File, do you mean?" Under other circumstances he would have loved her way with the language, but not now. Where in the hell had she heard this?

"I mean who I mean," she said, standing in the middle of the room facing him. "I have people who tell me things. You are not the only person. Damn! I have told you that many, many times!" She stopped, her eyes narrow as she seemed to appraise him. "Men is a fool, I do not like."

"I know, Carla, but you have told me that you like me." Cole Diamond's oily smile had spread into his voice and his excitement quickened as he saw her disdain.

"I want this Gunsmith. I have told you that? But why you don't listen? I meet him. I see him. He is not the most fastest gun. Not!"

"My dear, I of course will not lie to you. I have sent for John File in order to—uh—equalize our situation here with Adams. You can still shoot Adams if you want to, or anybody else. Except—of course myself." And he gave a laugh at that, to cover the flush he felt coming into his face as she stared at him.

Suddenly her whole mood changed. Imperceptibly, at first, she softened. She even appeared to melt. Her shoulders let go, she shifted her stance just enough to release the rigidity that planted her right in the middle of the floor, her lips moved as she ran the tip of her tongue between them.

Diamond felt his organ stiffen. He knew these shifting moods of hers. He knew it was tactical. But why not? He was not afraid of her, only ravenously desirous of her fantastic favors.

She had been wearing riding gloves and now, with her pelvis pushed slightly forward, her lips parted, and her eyes directly on his mouth, his chin, then back to his mouth as she pulled off one glove and, with a very light flick, struck him on the cheek; now with her white teeth showing on her lower lip.

Cole Diamond thought his trousers would split.

"I want first shot with Adams," she said.

"But, my dear, he could very possibly kill you."

"He will not. I know this men. I know where he is weak. I saw him, spoke with him. I know how to get him. And even so I am the fast one. Faster, fastest. You will see."

She had pulled on her glove again. And her eyes dropped to the bulge in his trousers. "You understand this, Cole. I want Fill not to get in my way. You promise that or . . ."

Her eyes were gleaming as she looked at him and then returned to his trousers.

"I'd better lock the door," Cole Diamond said.

"First you give your word!"

"Of course," he said, his breath tight in his chest. "Of course, I'll lock the door."

But she blocked his way as he started to move. Her body was right up against his and her gloved hand reached down and pressed on his erect organ. "Why lock? I like it to not know surprise if some person opens."

But he broke away and stepped swiftly to the door and locked it. He turned back to face her laughter.

"Men! What fool you are. I not care. But you—you are like old lady!"

But Cole was not to be dissuaded by argument or even insult. He had already unbuttoned his trousers.

"Why you do not let me?"

And now she was right up against him, pressing her body against his, her legs apart, while at the same time she reached down and pulled his erection out of his pants.

"Oh God," he murmured as, gripping it, she dropped to her knees, holding him tight now as her tongue flicked out and licked the head of his penis.

She blew on it, teased it with the tip of her tongue, slid it only a little way between her lips, teasing it to even greater rigidity.

He had somehow managed to grab a chair and pull it over so he could sit down, for he was too weak to remain standing. And now, with his legs wide, his pants pulled down well out of the way, she took him deep into her mouth, working slowly—expertly—all the way along his shaft with both mouth and hands, teasing his balls, biting him just enough to bring near-explosion, but then stopping and in an instant beginning fresh delights, until at last he could control himself no longer and he came totally, as she sucked and stroked, and drank him.

They remained still for a moment, Cole totally spent, his organ limp, while she continued to play lightly with the inside of his thighs, his belly, his balls.

"I don't have any more," he said at last. "My God, you took it all."

"Don't lie," she said. "See how you lie, Cole; he is already growing." She gave the tip of his organ a quick little kiss and looked up at him. He had been watching her every move. "I can make him big any time I want," she said.

Sitting back on her heels now and releasing him she started then to get up.

"No! My God, Carla."

She gave a little laugh. "What—no?"

"You can't leave me high and dry. I want more."

"But you said there was no more."

"Not true. There's more."

"All the time you lie, Cole."

"You're irresistible. No man can withstand you!"

"I know that!"

He had put his hands around her head to pull her down to him, but she pulled back.

"What about Joe Fly?"

This time he didn't correct her to play the game. "I told you, you get first crack at Adams."

"But you lie. We just see that."

"Not about that. I tell you, you get first shot."

"You promise!"

"I promise."

And now as she came down on him, her fingers teasing just ahead of her lips, he said, "Carla, take your gloves off this time."

THIRTEEN

Clint was up early. The sun was not yet at the horizon though the sky at the edge of the distant mountain tops was beginning to lighten. He was still thinking of Carla Onterra and her singular exhibition of shooting the day before. There was no question but that she was a real handful for any man who would wish to tangle with her. Clint had no such desire as far as any involvement could go, but he knew very well the promptings in his body which had been so strongly present when they'd been talking. Only there was business at hand and so he saddled Duke quickly after he'd boiled up some coffee for himself. The sun was just tipping the horizon as he rode out. He had decided that the first thing to do was check Marsh Cantwell's place for any sample of his handwriting that would help to establish the authenticity of the signature on the quitclaim deed at the Land Office. But on his way he took time to cover the approaches to Buzz Fahnstock's homestead, looking for sign of anyone who might be watching the place. He did find tracks of two shod horses near the creek directly south of the main house, and he followed them as they led away from the Fahnstock land until they simply disappeared in the desert.

He was about to give up at the point where he had made a complete circle around the ranch when something caught his eye just in the shadow of a big rock. By now the sun was halfway up to the center of the sky; the middle of the forenoon and hot. Clint was aware of it baking into his back as he swung down from Duke and approached the unusual object. And once again it was a matchbox with a piece torn out of it; just like the one he'd found on the night of the fire. He was pretty sure now that it was a plant. Nobody in their right mind would be so inattentive as to leave such a giveaway lying about. Admittedly, it could have happened accidentally at the site of the fire, due to excitement and the fact that he and Buzz were close by. Haste, and concern over getting away without being discovered could account for such a lapse at that time. But not now. Someone had been scouting the area, watching the house, possibly even setting up or planning a future killing. Anybody in that line of business would be that much more careful about leaving sign. Furthermore, there were no horse tracks even though the ground was relatively soft, nor any boot tracks. He was sure the matchbox had been dropped there to suggest that it was somebody else who was guilty of the fire. Or, it didn't have to be a "somebody else." The matches could have been dropped both times simply in order to confuse.

He rode on toward Cantwell's homestead without deciding one way or the other about the matchboxes; nor seeing any untoward sign or even seeing a single man or horse. And he was just remembering that not only had Marsh Cantwell's body disappeared but so had his dun horse, when suddenly breaking through a thick stand of cottonwoods near a creek he saw something lying on the ground, half in the water and half on land. It was the dun horse, and there was a round bullet hole right through its forehead. There was a folded piece of paper tied to the animal's ear.

Swiftly, Clint dismounted and, studying the body of the horse for a moment, decided it had been shot several days ago. He pulled the piece of paper free from the rawhide strip that was holding it, and unfolded it. The words were written in pencil, rather poorly.

Get out of here or take what you got coming to you.

Then he realized that because he had circled around again in search of tracks he was still on Buzz's land. So the note was definitely for Buzz, and the horse obviously a crude threat of what would happen if he didn't heed the warning.

It was getting toward mid-afternoon by the time he reached Cantwell's, for he'd spent time doing some more scouting on the way. The sun was still hot as he rode up to the house. He was surprised to see a saddled horse in the remaining corral; and was at once on his guard.

Suddenly the door opened and Marshal Abel Tymes stepped out.

Seeing Clint Adams he said nothing; possibly because his bony jaws were busy working over a big chew of tobacco. He paused now to eject a thick stream of spittle, tobacco, and a muffled curse in the direction of a clump of dried horse manure.

Clint told him about the dead horse and showed him the note.

"Looks like the boys are winding up," Tymes said. "I hear that one John File is about."

"Working for Diamond?" Clint suggested. He knew of John File, though he hadn't known the man was in that part of the country. He knew the man's reputation. After all, who didn't?

"You see what I mean about yourself?" Tymes was now saying, squinting at Clint from beneath his dirty, chewed-up Stetson hat. "See, trouble follows you, don't it." He said this matter-of-factly, with no complaint. For he had touched that way of life himself.

"You could have told me to ride on," Clint said.

"Sure, and the hare could've not stopped to take a piss so's he would of won his race with the tortoise," the marshal replied, reaching into his baggy pocket and bringing out a fresh plug of tobacco and a knife.

"He'll be after me," Clint said. "Same old story."

The marshal lifted his fresh cut of tobacco to his mouth, holding it on the blade of his knife with his thumb. He didn't answer for a moment, and then, his cheek bulging, he said, "They'll set you up for a back-shooting, Adams. File is a man who don't take chances. And Diamond is a sonofabitch."

"I guess you're glad I didn't take on your offer as deputy," Clint said with a wry grin.

"Adams, yourself or John File—one or the both—is going to be just as dead whether you take on as deputy or you don't. The offer is still open."

"Sorry, my friend."

Marshal Tymes said nothing to that. He spat, then

respat, and said, "What is your business here on the Cantwell homestead?"

Clint told him then about his conversation with Buzz Fahnstock and how he was there to find a sample of Marsh Cantwell's signature to check it against the signature on the quitclaim at the Land Office in Phoenix.

Tymes inclined his head in agreement at that, saying, "I been out here looking for anything that might be of use on the killing. Found nothing. No money; and he didn't make a deposit in the bank. If money passed hands he done something with it unusual. Usually it goes into the bank or it's cached. But I'll be damned if I can find it."

"Did you see anything with his signature on it?"

"I believe so. He's got a box full of papers there, and I do believe I saw something like that." He paused. "For the matter of that, I got a letter from Marsh, down to my office. I was figuring to take a trip to Phoenix myself to take a look at that writing."

Clint smiled at that. He was getting to like Tymes a lot. The marshal had his own ways, his own speed, and his own sense of humor.

"Then you saved me a search and a trip to Phoenix," Clint said.

"Glad to oblige," Abel Tymes said. "I'll be on my way," he added.

"Do you have any idea who does this to his matches?" Clint asked, showing Tymes the torn match box he'd found that morning, and telling him too about the box found at the site of the fire.

Tymes examined the torn matchbox and shook his head. "I'll let you know if I do," he said. And then, without another word, without even a nod he turned and walked toward the corral.

Clint waited. Presently Tymes returned leading his horse. When he had swung up into the saddle he walked the animal slowly toward Clint. "I'll be taking a look at that signature," he said, squinting down at the Gunsmith from his saddle, leaning on the pommel, chewing a little, Clint thought more for reflection than taste.

Without another word the marshal of Kilton Wells booted his horse into a fast walk which presently broke into a brisk canter.

Watching Abel Tymes cantering out of sight Clint was struck by the fact that while the lawman had inquired on his being out at the Cantwell Homestead, he had said nothing about the property now being Diamond's, until possibly proven otherwise. Yet, he knew Tymes was sharp, wouldn't have overlooked that fine point, and would have been as aware of its pointedness as he was himself. In other words, he was trespassing and legally Diamond or any of his hired men would have a right to shoot him if it came to that. And Tymes knew it.

Pondering on it, yet with his attention fully alert to his position in the surrounding country, he walked over to Duke and checked his rigging. Then he swung up into the saddle.

"Well, old fella—which way?" And he let the big black horse have his head.

After a while he found himself in a little valley just north of Cantwell's homestead. It was a lush valley, restful and isolated. Clint felt the need to think things through. There seemed no way either he or Buzz could rouse the other homesteaders to fight Diamond and his association of established stockgrowers who would themselves simply stay out of it and handle the whole thing through their hired guns, notably John File.

Finding a shaded spot near some trees, he dismounted and groundhitched Duke. Fully alert he moved into the protection of the trees and lay down, listening. He had found that lying absolutely still with his ear pressed to the ground was a good way to hear movement coming through from quite a distance. It was in fact the way the Indians did it. But he could hear nothing. He sat up now, and leaned against a tree, still completely alert.

And so the only answer that kept coming back to him was the one he didn't wish. Direct confrontation. The homesteaders weren't going to help Buzz, or even each other; and who wanted to go up against Cole Diamond's gunpower. Of the lot File, after all, was the best, the most dangerous, but Diamond's other gunmen were able professionals. And who knew how many more he could whistle up for action.

He had told Buzz that Diamond could strike at any moment now. He was only waiting for a pretext, something that would be able to satisfy the Law that the action he took would be justified. A simple matter to arrange. Like burning one of the association's brands on a calf, then changing it with a running iron to one of the homesteader brands; or even branding a few slicks, who would of course not be carrying any marking as yet, with a homesteader brand. And there were any number of other ways to frame it.

Clint had told Buzz that he reckoned Diamond was only waiting for the spring roundup, a good time for slipping in some fast and dubious action when there was a lot of activity and excitement in the air.

But the question was how to head it off. And in what way? Confrontation with the guns? That could be disastrous. Good as he was, Clint had no illusions about tak-

ing on a half dozen or more gunswifts, who most surely
would be backing John File every step of the way. So he
could shoot File, kill him, and himself be killed a half
dozen times over by Cole Diamond's gunhawks.

Yet, more and more, his thoughts began to circle
around Cole Diamond and the necessity of confrontation. And the girl, the girl with the jet-black hair and the
marvelous figure. Who was she? The name Carla Onterra meant nothing to him. She was not wearing a wed-
ding band so he assumed she was a single girl. Yet
anybody that attractive surely had a man. Perhaps in her
case—men.

Looking at the sun he realized it was getting late.
He'd have to take some kind of action soon, or at least
be ahead of Diamond's game, which would be the better
way to deal. Yes—it was suddenly clear now. Very
clear.

Quite plainly, Diamond and his partners were playing
a waiting game, waiting for the homesteaders simply to
break apart, which they were already doing, except for
Cantwell, who had paid with his death. And also except
for Buzz Fahnstock, who was alive. Still alive. Was he?

Clint was filled with sudden foreboding as he
mounted Duke and headed back to the TeaKettle. It had
been obvious for some time that Buzz was to be the next
target for the cattlemen—the dead dun horse and the
note surely pointed to this. It was obvious too that
Clint's appearance on the scene had altered Diamond's
plan. But now John File had come. John File was sup-
posedly the equalizer. Which meant that the plan could
go ahead. Buzz was clearly the next target. Clint lifted
the big black horse into a gallop as the feeling of foreboding grew in him.

FOURTEEN

The night was strangely quiet. Clint noted that no coyotes were howling, which sometimes meant they had detected the presence of people in the region. The only sounds came from the crickets.

An uneasy feeling of impending danger suddenly swept over the Gunsmith, and he turned his head abruptly to fix his eyes on the area of the corral. He was sitting on the porch of Buzz Fahnstock's house. He'd been surprised on returning from Cantwell's place to find Buzz not at home, then he'd seen the note saying that he'd gone into town and would be back the next day. Clint had grinned at that, knowing full well how horny a man could get lying around recuperating. And Buzz Fahnstock had always been a man who never hesitated to indulge his sexual appetite. There was no sign of Wendy. For a moment he wondered if she was with Buzz. He didn't feel the slightest twinge of jealousy, only idle curiousity. She had moved her things down from her place, and made herself at home, it seemed. Then he remembered that she had mentioned riding into Kilton Wells to buy a few supplies that were needed.

Feeling slightly restless, and also experiencing a premonition of mounting trouble, he had walked outside to sit down and take a look at the stars and try to figure out a way to stop Cole Diamond and his men, and also how to deal with John File, not to mention the "mystery lady," who he was now convinced had shot at him.

He had sat there watching the moon come up. But there was still the scent of Buzz's burned barn in the air, though he needed no reminder really to know that the big trouble was coming soon and that when it came it would hit fast, and more than likely in a totally unexpected manner.

Now the moon was high and he suddenly noted objects in the field of his vision that he'd not seen before by moonlight. There were three rather dim outlines, like stumps; but he knew well enough they were not stumps, for he was fully aware that no trees that would leave stumps like that would ever have grown there in that particular place.

The Gunsmith's right hand slipped down the leg of his chair until it reached the Winchester rifle that lay close beside him. His fingers closed around it and he lifted it very slowly to his shoulder, not making a sound.

Buzz Fahnstock's dog Sonny, who had been lying nearby, now stirred. He had been dozing and was now fully awake, sniffing the air. All at once he growled. Instantly the three figures that had appeared to be stumps disappeared by flattening themselves on the ground. Sonny leaped toward them, barking savagely. A shot cracked through the dark and a cry of sudden pain came immediately from the dog. The barking stopped.

Clint stepped quickly to the side of the house and leveled the Winchester, leaving only one shoulder and a part of his face exposed. He had seen the flash of the rifle and had not taken his eyes off the spot, so that he was able to sight the piece as accurately as one could in moonlight.

Seconds after the gun barked, another rifle flashed from the corral, and a second gun of much smaller caliber barked from some bushes beyond a strip of grass. Clint fired at the last flash just as the bullet hit the side of the stone house and dusted him with rock chips.

The next shot was from the far end of the corral. Clint aimed at the flash and fired. He was instantly aware of the fact that one of Fahnstock's horses had come out of the corral, frightened by the shooting, and was now directly in the line of fire. Quickly, Clint bent down, found some small stones, and threw them at the horse. They hit the animal and sent it trotting away from danger. But Clint's movement had drawn fire, and a bullet cut awfully close; he later saw it had gone through his shirt-sleeve.

Without a moment's hesitation he answered the shot, and was glad to hear a cry of pain followed by cursing. Then all sound died away. There was no sign of Buzz's dog, Sonny. About ten minutes passed, and then he heard a clatter of hoofbeats beyond the corral, indicating that the attackers were withdrawing.

The Gunsmith was cautious. He stretched out on the ground, his rifle ready, and lay there for several minutes just listening. He whistled for Sonny, and heard a faint sound like a whimper. Finally, he crawled forward on his hands and knees and rescued the dog. He took him into the house, and was relieved to find that his wound was superficial. He washed it and applied some salve; and Sonny licked his hand.

The night ticked away endlessly while the moon reached its zenith and then dipped toward the western range of mountains. Fahnstock's other saddle horse at length wandered back to the corral, accompanied now by another horse, saddled and bridled but riderless. Clint figured one of his bullets must have scored, but he had no wish to go looking for the man in the darkness.

Finally, when the dawn came, he went into the house and boiled some coffee and drank it quickly, all the while keeping his eyes on the window and the yard outside the house. Then he went out and caught Buzz's horse and shut him in the corral, for the animal had wandered out again. Then he roped the strange riderless horse. The animal was bearing a Mexican saddle, and its headstall was also Mexican.

It didn't take him long to find the dead Mexican. He was lying flat on his back with his arms outflung. Beneath him was a .44 caliber rifle. He looked to be in his late thirties, and was dressed like a peon. Clint's bullet had hit him in the throat.

Presently he saw the hoofprints of two horses who were clearly running away from the corral. So there had to be three men in the attack party. He found an old tarpaulin on the ground outside of where the barn had been and covered the Mexican's body. There was no time to do more than that, for his plan had formed rapidly. Then he saddled Duke and leaving the Mexican's horse to find its own way, he rode out heading in the direction taken by the two surviving attackers.

He followed the trail of the men who had tried to kill

him until he was satisfied that they were heading for
Cole Diamond's place. Drawing rein by a clump of
mesquite on a high knoll he looked down at the two
spots moving quickly across the flat land and now heading north, away from Cole Diamond's Double D. Still,
they could have come from any of the other cattlemen in
league with Diamond.

The question that was in his mind now was whether
they had been gunning for him or for Buzz Fahnstock.
And suddenly he was thinking of the old hostler who
had taken the slug in his back at the livery in Kilton
Wells. He had that same question still: had that bullet
been meant for him, and not the man named Clay Tolliver?

Realizing he was no closer to an answer to either
question he turned his horse, lifting the reins slightly to
start him into a fast walk back down the trail he had just
come on. There was something nagging at the back of
his mind. And again he felt the uneasiness he'd felt
when he'd left Cantwell's place after talking to Abel
Tymes.

On a hunch he decided to take a different trail back
to Buzz's homestead. The hunch was a strong one and
he knew better than to go against it. So he took the right
branch of the trail that forked just before it reached a
stand of cottonwood trees.

Rounding a cutbank with the sun beating down onto
his head, his shoulders, the backs of his bare hands as
he held the reins, he suddenly caught the clipped sound
of gunfire. Duke had heard it; the big black's ears
moved straight up and forward.

"What is it, fella?"

He drew rein and sat absolutely still in the stock saddle. There was something different about the shooting. And then he realized what it was. Someone was shooting at a target.

Checking the terrain carefully he realized that they had ridden a half circle so that they had come up closer to Cole Diamond's place. He knew from the description that Buzz had given him that the ranch house was close. Curious, he walked Duke carefully toward the sound of the pistol shooting. It was coming from the other side of some high bushes that bordered a stand of cottonwoods along the bank of a creek.

Rounding the bushes he kneed Duke through an opening in the trees and waded the thin creek. On the other side he stepped down in the protection of more cottonwoods and groundhitched Duke. The shots were louder now. Checking carefully that there was no one about, he walked down a narrow trail to where it opened onto a small clearing. He knew who it was now.

This time she was dressed all in black—a split corduroy riding skirt and a loose silk blouse which was thoroughly effective in setting off the upper part of her figure. He was looking at her back now as she turned again to face the row of bottles on the fence that had obviously been constructed for the purpose. He could tell by the way she moved that she was thoroughly pleased with herself, proud of her ability to shoot the bottles. And there was no question now that she was good, really good.

Having demolished the row of six bottles in rapid succession she now turned toward three more bottles which were hanging from whang strings tied to the branches of two trees. This time she drew both guns and, shooting first with the right, then the left, and the right again, she smashed each bottle. Her draw was fast, and she didn't rush it.

After the shooting she stood still, slipping her two Colts back into the buscadero holsters slowly, obviously satisfied. He watched her as now she turned her attention to two new targets, a front and a sideview of a human figure, both nailed to a big board.

But the Gunsmith had also seen something else. He was just trying to formulate what he had seen—a hunch of some kind, was it?—when the girl turned. Her surprise at his being there was genuine. She raised her eyebrows, her mouth softened just a little.

"I feel someone watch me," she said. "That is why I shoot so well. I know it is the Great Gunsmith."

"Don't try sassing me, young lady," Clint said with a smile. "I agree it was good shooting."

"It was great, Mr. Adams."

"For target shooting it was good. I'd even say very good. For target shooting."

She threw back her head and laughed, revealing her long white throat as her silk scarf opened loosely.

"Mr. Adams. Let me see you do better."

"I think I told you that I don't do target shooting. For me the gun isn't a toy."

"You have killed a lot of men?"

"I've shot men, but only when it was necessary." He paused, measuring her with his glance. "And you. Have you killed men?"

It was then as she hesitated that he saw something flick into her eyes.

"No, only a boy or two, pretending to be men," she said, and her eyes went past him for just a second, and then returned.

The Gunsmith, keeping his hands well away from his sides, especially his gun hand, turned slowly to face the two men who were standing at the edge of the bushes.

"So we meet again, Adams," Cole Diamond said easily as he walked forward. "Come along, Lije," he said to his companion, "and meet the Gunsmith."

Clint could see the girl out of the side of his eye. He had heard the men approaching through the bushes, had listened as they dismounted their horses, and he could tell they were not bushwhackers. They were much too noisy. Even so, he kept himself almost in front of the girl, so that should anyone think of firing, they would realize she was in line as a target. Of course, Diamond was not carrying a gun, unless he had a hideout. And the other man with his big potbelly and heavy walk was obviously no gunswift. He carried a six-gun, but Clint could see it was more ornament than the necessary function of a man who lived by his gun.

"Like you to meet Lije Millerby, Adams. Lije is a member of the Stockmen's Association which we've got organized here to stamp out the rustlers." In spite of his stern look he was unable to keep his eyes wholly away from Carla who was busily reloading her six-guns.

"Carla, my dear, of course you remember Lije."

She raised her head, smiling coolly at Millerby. "With pleasure," she said.

And Clint watched the man's face color a little, though he wasn't sure whether it was in knowledge or in hopeful anticipation. The girl did look ravishing.

"My job offer is still open, Adams," Diamond said.

"And *my* offer is still open," Carla said suddenly, holstering the gun that she'd been loading and looking directly at Clint.

Clint Adams almost broke out laughing as he saw the

expression of astonishment on Cole Diamond's face.

"Your offer, Carla?"

"My offer for Mr. Adams to work on my gun, for sliphammer it."

"I'm pretty busy right now, Carla," Clint said agreeably. "But maybe later." And touching the brim of his hat he mounted Duke and looked down at the two men. "I think Buzz Fahnstock's the man you want to talk to, Diamond. Me, I'm just a friend passing through. Or—" he added, as though it had just occurred to him, "perhaps Abel Tymes."

"Tymes! What the hell for!" Diamond snapped out. "What has that old fool got to do with anything?"

"He is the law," Clint said, hard, and he was holding his eyes straight on Cole Diamond. "I think it's time you men talked to Fahnstock and the other homesteaders and the law. You can work something out."

"Those men have been stealing cattle, even, some say, rustling a horse here and there. I wouldn't have anything to do with 'em expecting to be shut of 'em!" Diamond shook his big head in emphasis of those strong words.

"Suit yourself," Clint said, turning Duke away from them. But then he looked back at the girl. "I might think about that sliphammer job if you want to bring it around."

Then, without a second look at the two men, he lifted Duke quickly to a brisk canter. He could feel the three of them watching his back as he left. He could feel Diamond's jealousy. And he had the strong feeling that he needed to get back to the TeaKettle. Yet he was glad he'd made the detour. First because of seeing the girl again; and second, to see her intoxication with pistol shooting. It gave him a funny feeling deep in his gut.

He'd only known a few—maybe a half dozen—women who carried guns and knew how to use them, and none of them looked like Carla Onterra. Nor did any of them appear to have the passion for guns that she had. They carried guns as a means of livelihood. Two who'd been in the Brown Hole gang, two who'd been gamblers, and another who robbed banks with her husband. None of them were beautiful, and none of them revealed the competitiveness that the dark-haired beauty did, an ambition that seemed very much out of place. So he was thinking as he rode down into Buzz Fahnstock's homestead. But he knew too that he wanted to know more. He had seen something about her when she was shooting the bottles and he wasn't exactly sure what it was. Yet he knew it was there and that sooner or later it would focus. He knew it was important. Maybe very important. But he knew that he had to be patient and not force it to come to him. Otherwise it would be lost.

At the same time he knew that he wanted to see her again. He knew she wanted that. Her attraction to him was as strong as his for her, he knew. It was only a matter of time and place; of opportunity. For there was Cole Diamond. And Clint Adams knew, as clearly as he knew the weather at any given moment, that here was a man riddled with desire and jealousy. Carla Onterra was without doubt a woman who could drive men to extremes.

FIFTEEN

He had ridden back to the TeaKettle to find that Buzz was still absent. Had he perhaps decided to stay over in town? Maybe he'd found something to alleviate his worries for a few moments. Well, if so, then good for him.

Nor was there any sign of Wendy. Had she decided to visit her ranch? Clint regretted now that he hadn't told her not to ride up to the Box T alone. But would Diamond and his partners—Lije Millerby, for instance—go so far as to hurt the girl? He wouldn't put it past a man like Diamond. Millerby? He wasn't ruling him out. He had read him pretty thoroughly back at Carla Onterra's target site. The man hadn't said a word, had simply kept his eyes on him, watching with a clear threat in his narrow face. Clint decided he wouldn't rule out anything as far as violence went in regard to Lije Millerby. And more than likely, the other members of the Associ-

ation would prove no sweeter. It gave him an odd, un-
pleasant feeling to think that the fight might possibly
lead to that vicious sort of violence. But Clint, for all
his still young years, was a realist. And he knew that in
the present mess he'd have to take every possibility into
account.

Only where did the girl Carla fit in? She really was a
mystery. He could easily imagine that she'd been hurt
by a man or men at an early age. But he didn't let that
thought sink very deeply into him. There could be other
reasons for her competitiveness and arrogance with
guns; yes, her willfulness and wish to dominate. And
with the kind of looks she had it would be easy for a
man to fall. And Clint wondered whether Cole Diamond's jealousy might not be turned to good advantage.
Why not?

To his surprise he was to see her sooner than he had
thought. He had decided to ride into town and perhaps
encounter Buzz along the way, or maybe Wendy; and
besides he felt the need to check things with Abel
Tymes. The marshal might not have gone to Phoenix
yet, and in any case he would likely be back in a day or
two if he had. Clint left that open as an option. He also
wanted to listen around a bit. No knowing what a man
could pick up here and there, in a saloon, the barber
shop and bath, or the local eatery. Men liked to talk; and
even if he were close-mouthed a man often gave himself
away with his expression, with the kind of silence he
was keeping. And in fact he did pick up something right
off—and he wasn't too surprised.

When he walked into the dining room of Kilton
Wells' only hotel—the Metropole—he saw her instantly. She was seated alone in a corner, partly con-

cealed by one of the big pillars that supported the high ceiling of the room.

As he crossed the big room—with maybe a dozen people at tables during the noon time—he knew that she had spotted him, even though she pretended to be engrossed in her cup of coffee.

She wasn't wholly successful with her smile when she looked up at his greeting. For an instant he had the feeling she'd expected him. Or—was it just chance? The question flitted into his mind, but he decided to deal with that later.

"What a surprise." And her smile, which he had the feeling had been practiced, slipped into a warmth that was more genuine.

"Might I join you?" Clint said.

"Please do."

Dropping his hat onto a third chair, he grinned at her, deciding now to take the strong approach.

"It's always nice to be expected," he said cheerfully.

Carla threw back her head and laughed. Her eyes were dancing as she looked right at him with the most naked passion he thought he'd ever seen.

"And why not, amigo? I know what I want and when I want it, and so I get it."

"You always get what you want?"

"I want you to came here, and you come. You see? It is simple." And her eyes were on his lips as she finished, her voice trailing into a huskiness.

"Well, it sounds interesting," he said lightly, feeling his excitement pounding through his body. "But there is the matter of coincidence."

"I not understand. All I am telling you is what happens. Carla wants, Carla gets."

"I see you've got Cole Diamond," Clint observed, making his voice casual, yet also lining the saloon gossip he'd heard with firmness. He had no intention of letting her think she was getting away with anything as far as he was concerned.

She had been leaning toward him a little, and now as the waiter came and took his order, she leaned back. A short moment passed while she looked down at her hands which were folded in front of her on the table.

She said, "Cole? He is—hmm—a friend. An amigo. I do not love him."

"Do you love anybody, Carla?" And Clint felt his erection driving into his trousers as he held his eyes on her lower lip which she was biting very lightly with her very white teeth.

"I love—love." And she burst out laughing, throwing her head back again.

For a moment he thought the top button on her taut blouse was going to burst open as her firm breasts drove against it. But it held. She was watching his eyes now as they felt over her.

"And you—do you love a person? I not care. You could love hundred womens, but I would make you love Carla."

Clint decided that it had gone far enough. He leaned forward on the table, holding her with his eyes now. "Look, Carla. I am attracted to you. I would wish to go to bed with you—lie down with you. But only because you attract me physically. Now if I attract you—you like me physically—then let's go. But I don't go for all this power stuff where you think you're God Almighty. I don't want sex with the Deity."

He watched the shock whip into her face and for a moment he half expected an outburst. But the volley that came forth was not one of anger but of denial.

"Friend, Clint—I not know what you say to me. I speak good English, but you make fun."

"No I don't. Strange to say, I can see myself growing fond of you, Carla. But you need some growing up. Maybe you need a man like Cole Diamond or," he added, "Lije Millerby, but not me. Leastways, not right now. I'm sorry." And he pushed back his chair and stood up.

For an instant he thought she was going to explode in fury. But to his surprise he saw only the tears standing in her eyes. A trick? Another ruse to get her way? But he felt sure there was something else there. Even so, he didn't stay to find out.

And still with the image of the tears standing in her eyes he turned on his heel and left the room.

In the lobby he ran into Buzz.

"This is my day for coincidence," he said.

"I heard you were in town, Clint. So took a chance on the Metropole."

"Any news of Wendy?"

"None. But I don't expect any. Why—should I?"

But Clint didn't answer that; instead he told Buzz about Cantwell's dead dun horse and showed him the note.

They soon made their way to the Double Eagle and, finding a table in the corner of the big room, began to talk. Clint was delighted to find his friend hale and hearty, yet somehow the feeling of oppression had not left him, not even now when he actually saw Buzz in the flesh.

And he realized that he was worried about Wendy.

"What about Tymes?" Buzz asked after Clint told of his encounter with the marshal out at Cantwell's homestead. "Do you get a notion he's with us?"

"I have a feeling he is," Clint said slowly, as he felt through his reactions to the meeting with Tymes. "But at the same time, he's trying to be legal. He has got to know what Diamond and the others are doing, but he needs proof." He leaned back in his chair looking up at the ceiling. "He might find it in Phoenix."

Buzz caught the ominous note in his friend's voice. "I'm damn glad we never let Wendy go to Phoenix to compare Cantwell's signature."

"There was never any question about that, my friend," said Clint. "But at the time she was all hot for your not going, and so wanted to go herself. It was all right to go along with that as long as it didn't get into action. It quietened her worries over yourself, and we didn't have a war on our hands. But you know neither of us would have let her actually go there."

Buzz was grinning. "You know a lot about women, Clint. I give you that, along with a whole lot else, by God."

"I believe I know a little something about men too, Buzz. At least, I hope so. I had damn well better in this business I'm in."

And they both joined in a chuckle over that.

Later, after they'd had another round of beer, Buzz said he was planning on spending another night in town.

"Something special?" Clint asked with a grin.

"Huh—could be. I'll let you know. But—uh—have you had any further action with that senorita with the six-guns?"

"Not anything that amounts to anything," Clint said. "But I might give it some thought. What interests me most is her connection with Diamond. And whether or not she was the one who took a shot at me, and maybe fired your place."

When they parted, Clint headed back to the Metropole. His thoughts were filled with Carla Onterra. It wasn't easy to think clearly about her. Her streak of cruelty was quite apparent to the Gunsmith, and so was her tremendous drive for power, her need to be first, best, and her attitude toward men. He wondered how she fared with Diamond, or maybe it would have been better to put it, how Diamond fared with her. Was she the power at the Double D? Somehow, he could not see her as simply a bed companion for Diamond. A woman with her drive and ambition wouldn't be satisfied with that role. She'd want, she'd demand more. But had she gotten it? It was a question that stuck with him during his walk back to the Metropole.

And it was in the next few minutes that one of the big shocks of his life—and indeed, one of the most delightful—suddenly struck him.

The desk clerk, a youth with a rather sneaky demeanor and shifty eyes informed him that he had a guest in his room.

"What kind of a guest?" Clint demanded. "And why did you let someone go upstairs?"

The young man's jaw fell open like a trapdoor in his dismay. "B-but, i-it-it's a-a w-w-woman," he finally blurted out. "It-it w-w-w-was a surprise . . ."

"It's only me," said the voice behind him. And to his relief—he had thought for a wild moment it was Carla Onterra—he turned to face a beaming Wendy. "It isn't Harold's fault. It's mine. I told him it was your birthday and I wanted to surprise you."

Clint was laughing both with relief and happiness at

seeing her. "You know, I was beginning to worry about you," he said, pretending schoolteacher severity, "I hadn't seen you in quite a spell."

"It just so happens, Mister Adams, sir, that I have not seen you either—uh—" And imitating his voice and manner, "in—uh—quite a spell."

They both burst out laughing, and even Harold found a smile on his tired face as he watched them move toward the stairs. In his head he was already speaking to Mr. Adams the next day, telling him that since the lady stayed overnight in his room that there would be an extra charge on his bill.

As for Clint Adams, the voice in his head was telling him that life couldn't have been sweeter. Just at the moment when he was wondering if he would be able to do something effective about his handling of the situation with Cole Diamond and company and how he could help his friend Buzz, help had come in the form of sex and relaxation. It was obvious what he needed to clear his head of his turning thoughts, and clear himself, too, for action.

There was of course only one way to go. And that's where they both went—just as soon as they had entered his room and he locked the door.

SIXTEEN

In the back room of the Double Eagle, which served as Cole Diamond's office in town, the five men sat around the green baize tabletop while a cloud of tobacco smoke drifted indolently to the high ceiling. It was a warm day and some of the men had sweat around their collars. Others were slightly red in the face. They had been drinking, but not to excess, only the customary social drink which they invariably indulged in when they met together as members of the Stockgrowers Association. Hot or no, all were in a good frame of mind for having at last reached the decision that they felt would bring to a climax and final solution the problem of the squatters in Big Tom Valley.

Cole Diamond in particular was pleased, for, after all, it had been his plan that they were following.

"It'll be easy as rolling over" was how he had

103

summed up. "Those damn fool squatters won't be ready and we'll just run our cattle right through."

"But after branding," George Macklin added.

"'Course!" Diamond scowled at the obvious remark. Fool Macklin just wantin' to horn in on the good idea. "What else!"

"Suppose they get the wind of our starting the gather early?" a man asked. A tall man with long, saddle-colored cheeks. His name was Wes Monigan.

"No one is going to get the wind of it, Wes," Lije Millerby said, staring hard at the speaker. "Unless it is from one of us here." And Lije glared around the table at the group, his eyes resting for a moment on each one, save of course Cole Diamond. Besides himself and Cole, there was Macklin, Wes, and a stocky man with graying hair at the temples named Grim. Harry Grim ran about a thousand head of good he-stuff up north above the Quinn place and he had a special problem. And he brought his problem once again to the group, right now as they partook of their drinks and began to relax. Harry Grim was not so relaxed or happy about the way things were turning out.

"What about the girl?" he was saying.

"Wendy Quinn, you're meaning." Wes Monigan leaned forward, his thick fingers loose on his glass of whiskey as he squinted across the table at Harry Grim.

"She is right in the way of my moving a herd up onto the mountain come summer. I have been telling you this, but I want it understood, by God, that this has got to be taken as a problem for the Association."

His hard words fell into the almost airless room and seemed to stay there. They didn't like it. They wanted to see it as Harry's problem, not the Association's. No one wanted to run counter to John Quinn's daughter, especially when John had died from bullets delivered by the Association's "regulators."

But Harry Grim, who was her closest neighbor, was once again reminding them of Wendy Quinn and how he was just not about to be the one to "take care of her." Thus far, the other four had grudgingly gone along with this. They were indeed an association to help each other, but no one wanted to mess with a woman, especially a young woman who was well liked in the country. And it was Harry, not the rest of them who would suffer her presence in the moving of stock. Only Harry had the particular problem. They were willing to help, even offer advice, but Harry was demanding active participation from the others.

He had turned now to Cole as he spoke of this particular problem. "Cole, this is the Association's problem. We agreed we were all in this thing together."

"Harry, don't worry about it. We'll work it out. Don't keep hanging on to it. We are all in together." Cole spoke with a soft urgency to calm his colleague.

"The five of us," Harry said, and from beneath his gray eyebrows he looked around the table, meeting nobody's gaze.

Cole was as reluctant as the others to get involved in what they all felt was Harry Grim's problem; but at the same time they needed Harry. And indeed, they had made the agreement—right here in this room by God and not so long ago—that they would hang in it together to run the damn squatters out of the country. Matter of fact, it was Cole's managing that had taken care of that damn fool Quinn who had been the loudest and most difficult of the squatters. Now, of course, it was Buzz Fahnstock.

"We'll work it out, Harry," Cole said, laying his

thick palms flat onto the baize tabletop. "We'll work it out." He pointed a stubby forefinger at Harry Grim's empty glass. "Another round." And he nodded to Lije Millerby to pass down the bottle.

Chairs scraped now as the men pushed back to stand, with Harry Grim finishing his drink as he rose. He gasped almost directly into the face of George Macklin who had been sitting beside him. Macklin didn't like it, Cole noticed, but said nothing.

Cole, however, was always pleased when he noticed little details about people. Macklin's aversion to alcohol, for instance, and Harry Grim's penchant for same. He had always maintained that given enough information on a man's habits, his likes and dislikes, you could play him like a fish on the end of a line. Cole took pleasure in this. And he was especially pleased with himself lately as he felt that he had amassed some pretty good information on the pros and cons of the love-of-his-life, the wondrous Carla, that creature with the body of a Venus, and the appetite and sexual daring of a devil.

As the men filed out of the room Cole's thoughts turned more fully to the wondrous Carla and, as always, he felt his hunger for her rising. He closed the door on the last man, turned back to the table, and poured himself a good shot of the special whiskey which was his own private stock—not sold over the bar outside, but offered only to special customers, and intimates.

He sat at the table, going over the plan that he had "suggested" to the Association, having first of all sounded each one out separately. When each had agreed, he had then brought it to the group, quite easily —a fact already established rather than a question to be discussed. It was so easy to handle them, he told himself now as his fingers fondled his glass, and a smile of good old honest self-satisfaction played on his lips.

He sat there a long time, his thought on the details of making an early spring roundup to surprise the homesteaders by grabbing off all the newborn stuff and slapping the Association's brands on them before any of the goddamn squatters could even get started. Range stuff. Free for the man's iron that got there the first. Well, by God, as he'd told the boys, they would get there the first and their—or—better, his—"regulators" would see to it that there was no trouble. And, by God, while about it, there was no reason why his real business should be even suspected.

He smiled down at the table now, across his big chest and belly. The plan was so beautifully simple. For wasn't it he, himself, Cole Diamond—Big King Cole —who did all the braining for the Association, who thought it all up, brought in the guns, including John File, did all the work, goddamn it! He deserved some of the squeezings! And by God, this time it was going to be more than just squeezings!

He took another drink, musing on his plan, yet with the edges of his thought reaching out toward the black-haired Carla in her tight pants—and without them too, by God! Cole had eaten heavily, as always, at dinnertime that is, at noon, and he was drowsy. His lids lowered under his great eyebrows, a snore rolled wetly out of his broad nose, his chin drooped.

The hard single knock on the door brought him right awake. One knock. The door opened and the tall, thin man walked in.

"Diamond?"

"I am Cole Diamond." He knew right away who the broad-shouldered man with the narrow hips on which rode the two low-holstered guns would be. No question. That single knock had announced it.

"Name is File."

"Take a seat." Cole pushed the bottle and a glass toward his visitor. Then he glanced toward the door which had opened following a tentative knock. "Well?"

The tone of exasperation fell like a smack against the embarrassed face of the bartender who said, "I told him I'd get you, Mr. Diamond. He just come right on in."

Cole scowled. "Next time do better," he said. "Remember that!"

As the door closed, Cole Diamond turned to the sardonic grin on his visitor's face. John File was already lifting his glass; a man who did not defer to ceremony but cut his own way through life. Cole was pleased. He'd put his bet on the right man.

"Glad to find you available," he said, leaning forward with his forearms on the table and lacing his fingers together.

"I am glad you have agreed to my price," John File said without any expression whatsoever on his long, bony face. His skin looked as though it had been stretched over his skull. Cole, who was not lacking in imagination, thought the man looked as though he had died and been brought back. And he felt something akin to a shudder pass through him. Without saying anything, he reached to his jacket that was lying on another chair and brought out an envelope and handed it to the man facing him.

"You'll find it all there," he said. "And as I wrote you, there's the possibility of a bonus."

"You mean when I get Adams."

"Let me put it this way. I really don't care whether you kill Adams or you don't. I'm only interested if he gets in the way. Then—there is extra for you. But if you don't have to kill him, why bother."

"He will get in the way," the other man said. "No worry on that."

Cole was playing it tight. He was thinking of Carla and his promise. Not that he had any intention of keeping his word to her. He didn't care who killed Clint Adams, just so long as he was taken out, because he fully agreed with File: Adams would be, indeed already was, in the way. But there was no need to say so, no need to lay out more money when, who knew, somebody else might take care of the Gunsmith. Hell, he might even drop dead of the croup! And this thought gave Cole Diamond a big, silent chuckle.

He could feel John File's hard eyes cutting into him. "I might be wanting a few things," the man said.

"Necessaries are to be expected."

The man, who looked like he was sewn together with whang leather, let his eyes move around the room, including the ceiling. "You own this here?"

Cole lifted his hand away from his glass in an offering gesture, while his big shoulders gave a slight shrug. "Some people think I do."

The other man's sharp teeth appeared in a sudden grin. "Good enough. I see you got girls upstairs."

"You can take your pick."

"Good enough." He stood, one thumb hooked in his gunbelt, while with his other hand he lifted and then drained his glass.

Cole Diamond's eyes were on the two black-handled guns that rode smoothly at his "range detective's" thighs. Each was tied down with whang leather. Snug. He was going to say something.

But File spoke first. "And drinks," he said.

"All you want. Except stay sober." Cole brought this in firmly. He wasn't afraid of John File. He knew his kind, had always kept clear of such, but had used gunmen from time to time. It didn't pay at all to show deference or fear. It didn't pay at all.

File grinned, and said, "Drink can kill you quicker than bullets. You think I'm a damn fool, for Christ sake!"

Cole knew it was time for flattery. "I was in Lead City. I saw you gun down at the Choctaw Kid. I never saw anything so fast."

John File had walked to the door. With his hand on the knob he turned. There was no expression on his face.

"Neither did the Kid."

SEVENTEEN

From her table by the window in the Metropole's dining room Carla Onterra watched the tall man dressed in black walking down the street. She saw heads turn, watched the surprise and awe in the faces of two young boys at the passing figure with its long, purposeful stride, its twin guns riding on those muscular thighs.

Carla knew those thighs well. And she thought of them now as she followed John File with her amber eyes sparkling. She thought of those hard thighs wrapped around her body, her head, and she felt again her passion rising for the man who had taunted her and spurned her. How long ago? She knew exactly, but at this moment of bitterness she refused to picture the scene. And then it came flooding in. The passion, the insatiable grappling in the beds, on the floors, on tables, chairs, standing up, out in the field, a couple of times in a creek, on a riverboat, in hotels and rooming houses, in wagons—anywhere and at anytime. It had been irresistible. Tremendous!

Until that day he had laughed at her. She had been practicing; a young girl still, eighteen. And in between the rides, the travels with him, without his knowing she had practiced. Practiced until she was good. Damn good! And then one day she had shown him. Had shown her accuracy, had shown her speed. And mostly she had shown her deadly calm. And he had laughed.

They'd had a few drinks and she'd worked up the nerve to show him. And in fact she had done well, shooting out the ace in three cards and then hitting the edge of a fourth which she had mounted sideways.

He hadn't been impressed at all at her "secret," which she had practiced for so long to surprise him and please him. He had simply laughed. They had been out in back of the cabin where they'd been staying, and she had set up a sort of target range. There were some bottles tied to a branch.

He had taken her gun and checked it. "Shoot the bottle," he said.

And she had done so with ease.

"Now shoot the string."

She had emptied her gun with no success. And then he had stood there, silent as death, and motionless. Not even breathing it seemed. Even now she wasn't sure she'd seen him draw his gun. Only the next thing she knew was he had shot the piece of whang leather that had held the bottle to the branch of the tree.

He had laughed. Again and again he had laughed. Remembering it, telling it to others, reminding her.

"You're just a woman, for Christ sake. You don't know how to shoot!"

And then the moment came when she'd found him with another woman. They were lying in a bedroll in the barn and quite by accident she had come in. She seemed to have gone blank right then, only she knew from piecing it together later that she had drawn her gun and he had—from his lying-down position—shot it out of her hand.

"Next time I'll kill you, you bitch!"

She was eighteen and he had laughed at her again and told his companion lying there beside him about her shooting. And she had started running. She had never seen him again, until this moment. And she knew it was the moment she had been preparing for, the moment she'd worked for, imagined and carried in her thoughts for how many years? It didn't matter. But she never stopped practicing. For—yes, ten years she had carried this resolve. Ten years as she came into her prime; while he, the famous John File, was growing older.

As he disappeared down the street her eyes still followed. She wondered if he knew she was in Kilton Wells. He'd find out soon enough. And what a coincidence Cole Diamond hiring him! She had covered her reaction well in front of Diamond, emphasizing that it was the Gunsmith that she wanted to kill, not letting on that she had ever known John File. Only that she was after killing the Gunsmith and becoming Number One. Well, why not both of them? John was past his peak. He had to be. She was sure he was. And in the back of her mind she knew too that she had indeed wished to gun down the Gunsmith so that he would hear of it. He would hear that she had outdrawn, outshot the Gunsmith, and by heaven or hell he'd have to face her then! How lucky he was right here in Kilton Wells. He might even see her shoot Adams!

But as she walked up the long stairway to her room she began to feel her passion mounting. Was it memory of those wild times with John? Or—or was it the way Clint Adams had looked at her, had felt her with his eyes. She wanted him. She wanted him really badly.

It was with this purpose in mind that she went back down to the desk and asked for the Gunsmith's room number. Five minutes later she slipped the note under his door. A simple invitation to supper.

As she passed the desk in the lobby once more she saw by the clock behind the desk clerk's head that it was getting on toward evening. Casually she looked about the lobby. Of course he wasn't there. But it was time for supper. People were entering the dining room. And to be sure, he might not come in, though the clerk had said he was still registered. Well, she would see.

She had only just ordered a cup of coffee to start with when she saw him walk in and head toward her. Ah, it was so good to have things work out the way she wanted! And for an instant she imagined Cole wondering where she was. She had her arrangements with him; he had to allow her freedom. Nevertheless, she knew how terribly jealous he was, and so was careful not to overstep the bounds of his jealousy. After all, Cole was a good provider. Much better than some others she'd had to put up with. And now, even as Clint Adams came closer, the thought flitted into her mind that perhaps John File might see them together. Although she also remembered from the past that John was a man who, when he was about his business, kept pretty much out of sight until the job was done.

Instantly she picked up on Clint's smile as he came up and said, "I got your note. Sorry, I have a date for supper. But perhaps another time."

She had smiled, and then he was gone. And she regretted that she had smiled. She wished she had simply regarded him coldly. Well, she reflected as she stood up, deciding she wasn't hungry after all, well, there was always Cole. Cole, she knew, was staying at the little office he kept in town; the room at the back of the Double Eagle. The only trouble was that it was the Gunsmith she wanted. And she had the strongest feeling that Clint Adams wanted her too. The feeling stayed with her all the way down to the Double Eagle.

She was disappointed again, for Cole had just left. There was a message in case she turned up that he would be back in a couple of hours, after attending to some business.

Irritable, frustrated, she walked back to the Metropole and entered the dining room. To her astonishment she saw Clint Adams sitting by himself across the room. He spotted her immediately and waved her over as he stood up.

"I concluded my business quicker than I'd thought," Clint said pleasantly. "Would you join me for supper, if you haven't already eaten and if you don't have some other engagement?"

"I would be delighted, senor. I thank you for your hospitable." And she sat down in the chair he drew out for her.

"I'd like some wine," Clint said. "How about you?"

"Wine! I love. Red, white—any. Red, white, blue wine—American!" And her laughter tinkled across the table.

She could feel her body tingling as he looked at her.

Then, as he signaled the waiter, her eyes cut across the room. A man was standing in the doorway looking in her direction. It was John File.

Carla felt absolutely radiant. Something in her told her that she had everything coming out just the way she wanted.

EIGHTEEN

Clint Adams had even felt after his session in bed with Wendy Quinn that he'd had his fill, at least for a while. The girl had been fantastic, as she always was. But now, less than twenty-four hours later he found, on encountering Carla Onterra whom he had spurned, that his passion had not only risen again, but was stronger than ever. He was delighted. Still, he would have refused the black-haired beauty again, and for the same reasons—her aggressiveness, her arrogance, her tremendous conceit—except that to his surprise he detected something different in her. He couldn't put his finger quite on it, but there was a sort of sadness about her eyes, a wistfulness, something very young; and it touched him. From the start he had been certain that her contempt and bullying behavior had been hiding something probably very painful to her; and from what he was observing now that seemed to be the case.

After replying to her note in person, while she sat
with her coffee in the Metropole dining room, he had
walked out to the street for some fresh air, wanting time
to think. He'd headed down to the Clean Whistle Saloon
and had a beer; and on returning to the street he'd seen
Carla entering the Double Eagle. She'd not seen him,
for which he was somehow glad. A few minutes later,
being hungry, he'd walked into the Metropole and ordered some supper. And it wasn't many minutes until,
to his great surprise, the girl walked in.

Facing her now across the table he had to admit that
her bragging about her looks and charm was certainly
justified. Only right now she wasn't bragging. There
was a quite different look in her face as she held him
with her eyes. And he was again surprised as she
dropped her eyes, almost shyly. Acting? He was not so
sure. There was that little girl somewhere close to the
surface. Now that he knew it he could spot it.

As they sat talking he watched her old confidence
returning, wondering what had caused the change in the
first place. He didn't mind. He had more than decided
or his body had—that she was utterly desirable, and the
stiffness of his sexual organ was a most potent reminder.

"You don't seem very hungry, Clint," she said with
her teasing smile as she bit into a piece of fruit which he
was happy to realize signaled that the meal was coming
to a close.

"It's your great beauty that drives ordinary hunger
away," he said. "You see, I feel that for you, so I don't
see any point in pretending otherwise."

"But don't you like to have fun in playing, Clint?"

"Of course. That's all part of it." And his eyes kin-
dled with the feeling that was sweeping through his

whole body. "Sure," he said. "I love to play. But not too much. There comes a moment when new action is called for. I'm sure you would agree with that."

She was biting her lower lip ever so lightly as she watched his mouth.

"I know just so; I am full and whole with the thing you say to me, Clint. I want you." Her smile broadened as she sat back in her chair, keeping her eyes on him. "I am longing for your—long one. How you say that?"

"You don't say it," he told her, pushing back his chair.

She didn't catch it at first, but then she giggled as he escorted her out of the dining room, with his erection making a tent of his trousers so that he had to carry his hat to cover it.

The moment the door was locked she melted against him, slipping her arms around him, her hands sliding down into his trousers, searching his buttocks, while he eagerly lifted her dress and began pulling down her drawers.

In only a moment they were naked and he was standing with his great erection between her legs, her great bush wet on him. Slipping her arms up around his neck she lifted herself up, spreading her legs wider and then settling down onto his organ to slide onto it as he stood there with buckled knees, nearly going out of his mind.

"Walk," she hissed at him. "Walk me!"

Clint was only too glad to oblige as he walked with his rigid cock all the way up into her as she wiggled fantastically, gasping with joy.

"Down on the floor!"

He let her down and she twisted away to go onto her hands and knees so that he could drive into her from the rear. She was soaking, and wide open as now she began to crawl over the floor on her hands and knees while he followed her with his plunging member, probing and sliding deeper and deeper until finally she came to a stop, whimpering with her exquisite pleasure, crying out small words of utter joy as together they danced his huge cock faster and faster until all at once he knew he had to give and he exploded just as he felt her come squirting onto the end of him and they sank hopelessly to the floor, turning toward each other and reaching for the embrace as, still coming, he entered her from the front and rode her high and hard and fast until he came once more and she bit his neck, dug her nails into his buttocks, and all but screamed into his ear as they flooded each other again.

Somehow they managed to crawl up onto the bed and sink again into each other's embrace.

They lay silently together with the odor of their sex filling the room. Clint felt totally relaxed and at peace.

After some more moments she turned toward him and he felt her breast in his face. So quickly and so hungrily had they come together that neither had had time to explore the other's body. But now they did. And Clint found her to be all that he could have imagined. Her breasts were firm and springy and fit his hands beautifully. The nipples were big, hard, and rosy. Her entire body seemed to ripple just beneath the skin with joy, and he found her mouth was as succulent as her lips between her legs.

She started to play with his balls now and instantly he was erect.

"I love you—this," she said, squeezing him, And, leaning over, she began teasing the head of his penis with her tongue. Meanwhile, he reached down and played his fingers in her vagina. Soon she had his whole organ in her mouth and was sucking.

He withdrew as she grabbed him and pulled him back. And this time he teased her by bringing it almost out, and then slowly, very slowly, lowering it down her throat.

She came up at last, gasping for air.

"He is one hell good cock!" she murmured as she ran her fingers along the line between his buttocks and now took his balls from the rear. Bending down again she opened her mouth wide for them, sucking them while stroking his member with her fist.

Now Clint turned her over, and spreading her legs wide, rode into her high as she squealed with utter delight, her buttocks bucking against the mattress as he brought her closer and closer; but then releasing it a little, he slowed, teasingly, then, as she gripped him with her nails and heels, he brought her up onto her shoulders, driving into her until she begged him to come. And he was most happy to oblige.

And not very long afterwards, he was still feeling happy as he came downstairs and parted company with her. In full view of the rather ordinary-looking man seated in one of the Metropole's big armchairs. With his shifty eyes and furtive posture he had Cole Diamond written all over him.

NINETEEN

While his time with Carla had been fantastic, Clint was certainly not about to lower his guard with her. Sure, there was the little girl inside whom he had seen peeping out with that yearning look, but he had also seen the cool, whipcord body draw and shoot, he had caught the contempt and anger in the words that came past those passionate lips. It was the day after they had bedded together that he remembered something he had half-noticed at Carla's target site, but it had slipped away, only touching the edge of his awareness. Yet it was there, it had made an impression, and it came back. Two targets, but barely noticed because of being partly hidden by the branches of some trees, had revealed the outline—front and profile—of a man's body. He had even noted the little holes that dotted them. Bullet holes. Yes, he remembered more clearly now as he concentrated on that impression; and the whole scene, the very moment, swept back and with it the feeling he'd had, that here was someone who indeed had a fixed thought, a truly hard resolve. Why?

For her other side, her passionate yearning for sex— and her ability moreover—belied a woman who was a cold-hearted killer. It was a mystery. But he knew he would have to handle it carefully. Clint knew he would definitely have to handle Carla Onterra carefully.

On a hunch he saddled Duke and, while intending to make for the TeaKettle to see if Buzz had made it back all right, he decided to take a swing over toward the Double D. He wasn't concerned that Buzz might still be in town, for he did have a man on the place, Clancy, a tall, rough-hewn Ohioan who worked both for Buzz and one of the neighbors. It was a good arrangement, giving Buzz time away from the outfit when he needed it. In no great hurry to get home, the Gunsmith pointed Duke toward the Double D and Carla Onterra's target site.

It was about the middle of the forenoon when he came down the gulley and around the cutbank that marked the border of Cole Diamond's property. He pulled up near a stand of mesquite, deciding to wait. He was in no hurry, for he knew how risky it was riding in at such a time, but to come in under cover of darkness would have served nothing. Diamond would of course have outriders and the question was how to get past them. On his last visit he'd been lucky, but now, having found him at the target site, Diamond would surely have warned his men to be on a sharp lookout.

Covered by the mesquite trees he squatted and studied the terrain. An hour passed, and he waited still longer until it was high noon. It was still chancy, but he knew that high noon was the time men grew drowsy,

were looking for some grub or a snooze in the shade,
and at such a time a man's eyesight wasn't as good as in
the early morning. It was a hot, slightly muggy day and
this could work to his advantage. He needed any help he
could muster.

He had seen no riders; yet still he waited. There had
to be somebody, he knew. And then, after another
quarter of an hour, he saw the horseman approaching
down below. Good. He was likely making his rounds,
just seeing that everything was as it should be. A lone
rider. There could be a follow-up man, and Clint waited
some more minutes to be sure. Then, seeing no one, he
checked Duke's rigging and stepped into the stirrup and
mounted. He rode carefully but quickly down to the
target site and slipped into the trees and dismounted,
groundhitching the big black and checking his weapons.

For several minutes he stood absolutely still, listening. He was listening not only with his ears, but with his
body. Overhead some geese flew, making no distur-
bance in the faint blue, heated sky. Clint remained absolutely still. Then, only when he was completely
satisfied, he started forward and in a few minutes he
was at the target site.

It was as he had remembered it: the bottles, some
still not broken, were stacked in a large pile. He imagined her getting her supply from Cole Diamond's Double Eagle. And there were the two targets. He spent
some time studying them.

Something was puzzling him as he looked at the two
figures, profile and straight on. But nothing came. He
only saw that her aim had been true. Head shots, throat,
chest, and belly. There were a few at the facing target's
gunhand.

He didn't linger. He had seen something, but he didn't know what it was. He was puzzled as he stood looking at the targets again. They were more than simple line drawings. The artist had drawn in some features. It was time to leave. The Gunsmith felt that strongly. He returned quickly to where he had left Duke and in another minute he was riding back the way he had come.

Now he had two puzzles. The figures on the targets seemed somehow vaguely familiar, yet for the life of him he couldn't say what that familiarity was. And then he still had that feeling of something he had noticed about the girl when she'd been shooting. He studied it again, and then dropped it. He was not a man to ruminate like a cow. He knew it would come to him if it was important. And he would simply have to wait.

When he got back to the TeaKettle he was met by a worried Wendy. Buzz had taken a turn for the worse and was in bed. But Clint found him awake when he walked into the room.

"You went and overdid it," he said, joshing his friend. "An old bugger like yourself has to handle those young girls easy like."

His friend's response was weak but there. "You ought to know, by God." But Buzz couldn't pull off the hearty laugh he tried.

"I've been missing you and Wendy all around," Clint said. "And now I feel it's time we dig in. I've got a heap big feeling heap big trouble is about to happen."

"It has," Wendy said, coming into the room with some water for Buzz.

Clint waited while his friend drank. It seemed to revive him, or maybe it was Wendy's words.

"Clint, the buggers are pulling an early gather, and they're fixing to run their stuff right through this valley."

"You mean, right through here."

Buzz had started to cough and Wendy took the half empty glass of water from him before he dropped it.

"We got the news just now," the girl said, looking at Clint with concern.

"That includes your place," Clint said.

She nodded.

"When will they actually start the roundup?"

"Any—any time," said Buzz from the bed, his voice wheezing out the words. "They'll brand all the slicks with the Association before we can do any separating. Everybody's beef will be in there. It's a showdown."

"You don't think maybe it's a rumor Diamond and his bunch might have planted?"

"Hell no."

"They're going to a lot of trouble," Clint pointed out. "Bringing in a man like John File, starting an early roundup, and maybe bringing in even more guns. They want it awfully bad."

"It's prime grazing country, Clint," the man in the bed told him, his voice slightly calmer now.

"I know that. But it seems to me there's something here that we're not seeing."

"What do you mean?" Wendy asked.

"They're trying too hard to scare you off. That's the feeling I get."

Buzz started to struggle to lift himself up onto his elbows and Wendy flew to his side.

"You stay down!"

But he ignored her. "What d'you mean?" he demanded, staring at Clint. "Those boys are not fooling around."

"I'm not saying they are fooling around," Clint insisted. "What I am saying is that they're doing an awful lot of fancy footwork. I do believe they're covering something."

It was just then they heard the horses. They were coming in fast. Buzz jerked up in bed. Clint was already at the front window. But by now it was dusk and hard to see who was approaching.

At the window, Clint tried to get a count on the riders. There were a good half dozen; it was hard to count in the fading light and the tangle of horsemen as they bore in at the gallop. He realized that behind him Buzz was getting up over Wendy's protests.

The cadre of riders pulled up in a cloud of dust, one of them bellowing out Buzz Fahnstock's name. He was evidently the leader.

"Fahnstock! Come on out. Or listen to this through the door—one!"

"Hand me that Winchester!" Buzz demanded, and from the side of his eye Clint saw the girl obey.

"What you want, you sons of bitches? State your business and get the hell off my land!"

Seeing him move to a window with the Winchester ready, Clint said, "Don't shoot. Even if they shoot, hold your fire."

He had started quickly into the kitchen, which was at the back of the house, telling Wendy to stay with Buzz and to do nothing, not even speak, until they heard from him.

Quickly he raised the window and slipped out, carrying his .44-.40 Winchester. It was almost dark, as he took a moment to fix his bearing before he began easing along the back of the building and around the corner to the side. And then he moved swiftly up to the corner of the house that met the front. He could hear the riders talking, with the leader taunting Buzz who now and again shouted at them to get off his land.

There was a water barrel at the corner of the building and Clint crouched behind it. Slipping the rifle barrel around so that the bunch at the front door were covered, he called out to the horsemen.

"You're covered. First man makes a move he is dead. Now turn your horses real easy like and haul yourselves out of here. I mean right now!"

"Adams—that you?" snapped the leader.

The Winchester cracked out and hit the corner of the porch post inches from the man who had spoken.

"That shot was intentional, mister. Next time it'll be right on target. I said—git!"

"Fuck you, Fahnstock!" Somebody screamed out as all of the riders spun their mounts and pounded out of the yard.

The Gunsmith waited till they were well away before he walked around to the front door and was let in by Wendy.

Buzz was standing in the middle of the room, his rifle in his hands, his breath coming shallow and fast.

"Now do you still believe they're not serious, Clint?"

"Buzz, I believe they're dead serious, but I think they're faking something."

Buzz shrugged, looking toward Wendy for help, with a puzzled smile on his face.

But Clint was paying no attention to either of them. He was standing quite still in the center of the room, his thoughts obviously on something that didn't include either of his friends.

"Just stay in here," he said, suddenly looking up. "Don't go outside."

"You got a notion?" Buzz said, catching on.

"Dunno. Just don't go out." And without saying anything further, he walked into the kitchen. "Turn the lights out," he said to Wendy as she followed him. "Like you were going to bed."

"Clint, be careful." She was looking at him earnestly and, despite the gravity of what he was thinking, he felt a tug at his heart. He put out his hand and laid it on her shoulder, then leaning toward her kissed her softly on the lips.

"Clint . . ."

He said nothing, but in the dark opened the back door of the house silently and slipped outside.

Silently he made his way toward the outhouse, stopping every few feet to make sure nothing had changed, that no untoward sound was coming from the little building. The going was slow, for even though there was no moon there was visibility and he had to stay close to the ground, taking advantage of any object he could find. When he was within a few feet of the wooden outhouse he stopped and, crouched low, listened. He could hear nothing unusual. Presently he began to circle around the building, moving with extreme care. It took a while, but his patience paid off when he smelled the horse. He stopped, absolutely still in his tracks, listening, not wanting to get any closer to the animal in case it would nicker. Now, choosing a line of approach that had some bushes to afford him cover he moved in closer to the outhouse. When he was within a few feet he stopped, and, feeling around, found some stones. Taking careful aim he threw them. They rattled hard against the little house and he suddenly let out a cowboy yell.

Dropping down instantly he rolled well away from the place where he had thrown the stones and yelled.

The rifle cracked through the night and he heard the man's horse whinny with fright. Then he saw him, silhouetted on top of the animal as he kicked it into a gallop, firing wildly back in the direction of the outhouse and the place where Clint had thrown the stones.

In one smooth movement the Gunsmith drew his Colt and, lining his shot perfectly, brought the would-be bushwhacker out of his saddle while his horse continued to gallop away.

It didn't take Clint long to find the man. He was dead. He pulled the body into a nearby shed that had escaped the fire, to leave it there till morning. Then he walked back to the house.

"What was all that about?" asked an excited Buzz Fahnstock.

"Just that I thought I heard more horses riding in than rode out," Clint said simply as he checked his handgun and reloaded it. "He was waiting in the outhouse, but then he must have gotten impatient and moved outside. Which was sensible actually, because inside there he was a dead target."

"Looks to me like he was a dead target no matter where he was," Buzz observed. And walking over to a chest in a corner of the room he opened it and brought out a bottle of whiskey. "I think we've earned us a drink."

"Phew!" said Wendy. "I think that will have to include me." And she looked over at Clint, smiling nervously.

He grinned at her, and reaching across the table ran his hand in her hair, tousling it. "You've earned it," he said.

And the three of them had a laugh at that.

Buzz raised his glass. "I am making a toast to my friend Clint Adams, and a promise to myself."

"Let's hear it," Wendy said.

Buzz was grinning ruefully, with his caught-in-the-act look all over his face. He nodded his head in salute, his glass still raised. "Here's to the best friend a man could have. Or—a woman," he added, glancing fondly at Wendy. "And here's to a damn fool who promises next time to listen to that friend when he warns him that everything ain't always just exactly what it looks like!"

Chuckling, they drank happily.

TWENTY

Abel Tymes lifted the pot of boiling coffee off the potbelly stove and poured the steaming liquid into his tin mug. He followed it with two big spoons of sugar and considered for a moment the possibility of adding some whiskey, but decided no, maybe later. He carried the mug of coffee over to the table that served as his desk, and sat down on the battered wooden chair. Al, the brindle cat who had appeared from nowhere one day soon after Abel had taken office, walked over and sat down and began licking his paw. Now and again he looked at the man seated at the desk, then, finished with his paw, he stood up, arched his back, stretched, and walked over to the pool of sunlight that lay on the floor just near the window. And lay down. After a moment he lifted his head and turned it to look at the man, and then lay back, eyes closed.

Marshal Abel Tymes noted those movements with no

interest whatsoever. He was thinking. And he was favoring his mug of coffee, without which life would have been difficult, though he would have managed. Tymes —going on seventy—got along with few necessities. He preferred it that way. His philosophy, if it could be called such, was that the less a man carried through life the less he'd have to get rid of when the going got tough.

Anyhow, the going was tough now. He had checked out Marsh Cantwell's signature at the Phoenix Land Office and had discovered what he'd suspected—that it was genuine enough to stand up before an impartial judge, and the clerk had agreed with him. Together they had compared the signature on the quitclaim deed with the sample that Tymes had brought with him. A handwriting expert might have found otherwise, but the clerk and the lawman agreed that the quitclaim signature had to look like the real thing. Though Abel Tymes had real doubt, yet nothing he could prove.

It was this that was occupying his thoughts as he watched Al the cat's maneuvers.

"Reckon you be wanting some milk," he observed, but he made no move toward the bottle that was standing on an upended crate near the stove. It was hot in the little room that was his office, and he shook off the drowsiness that began to seep through him and shifted in his chair.

He was stumped. With the signature authentic he didn't have anything legal to move on. He knew it was a forgery, it had to be, for he knew Cantwell's type. The man would never have signed over his place to Diamond. And where was the money? He'd checked the bank. Cantwell had made no deposit, in fact he hadn't even been in the bank since last winter. And where was his body? Tymes of course had suspected that Diamond wouldn't have been so crude as to not carefully fake the signature on the quitclaim. But now he was asking himself why it was he was simply assuming that Cole Diamond was the guilty party, and that Cole had faked the deed, had more than likely ordered Cantwell's murder. He sniffed. Well, hell, he knew Cole like he knew Cantwell. Knew the type. By God, he hadn't been a lawman all these years without learning something. He could read a man; and he'd sure had plenty of practice. He would put his money on Diamond being the guilty one. Cole for sure wouldn't have pulled the trigger. But he was behind it. He had ordered it. No doubt about that. No doubt at all.

And when the door opened and the tall man in the black silk shirt and California pants with the two tied-down guns walked in he knew he was right.

The only part of the marshal of Kilton Wells that moved as his visitor walked in was his eyes. They fastened plumb center on the man with the hard arms and legs.

"Some people knock," Abel Tymes said and lifted his mug of coffee to take a drink.

"I'm an old friend, Abel."

"You might be old, John, but you are not no friend of the law. Now state your business and then git."

"Are you ordering me out of town?" The smile was cold, pasted on the icy face. The eyes were like marbles. The man came closer, moving like a wound-up cat, Tymes thought as he saw Al move to take in the visitor then lower his head again.

"I am not ordering you out of town," Tymes said. His voice was firm, but he felt the tiredness in it as he spoke. "I've not lasted this long by being a damn fool." He shifted his weight now, facing John File more directly. "Tell me what you want."

"Just checking in," File said, "like any stranger passing through. Courtesy."

"Passing through?" Abel Tymes' tone was sour as a lemon. "Who you working for—as if I didn't know."

"Like always, for John File."

"'Course." The marshal sniffed, and turning his head, he spat briskly at the battered cuspidor which, though it was not very close by, he hit plumb center.

"What I am sayin', Abel, is I will only be about for a spell. Just long enough to like shake hands with a person. Then I'll be moseyin' on."

Abel Tymes blinked, then canted his head, squinting at the man with the two low-slung sidearms. "I am the law in this town, File. That means I keep the peace. Sometimes I got to go back so's the law can go forward —if you get what I am meaning. So I ain't telling you right now to drop those guns here on my desk; and I am not going up against you gun to gun. I am twice your age, and I am not a damn fool."

Suddenly Abel Tymes stood up. John File was surprised at how quickly his old acquaintance had moved. He watched as Abel Tymes walked to the gun cabinet that was standing against the wall behind his desk. He opened it, reached in, and took down a short, sawed-off Greener .12-gauge shotgun. He was holding it loosely by the barrel, making sure that nobody would mistake his intention.

The two men stood facing each other now, each knowing that hostilities had no place here at the moment.

"I am not planning on using this here, on account of I know you could cut me down before I got a finger on the trigger," Tymes said.

A thin smile was lining John File's lips as the marshal laid the ugly-looking gun on top of the desk.

"You be real fast, John. I honor that. But I am telling you this. You come into town any time from now on you leave them guns here or wherever. Do you understand me?"

A cold smile now moved through the other man's leathery face. "Abel, I am a man who minds the law."

"Good enough. On account of we both know that while you can outdraw me, this here..." And he pointed to the gun on the desk. "...this here can cut a man right in two at the pockets quickern' a cowpoke can unbutton his pants on a Saturday night."

In the silence that followed, Abel Tymes' visitor turned and walked to the door. He stopped for a moment with his hand on the knob.

"Good to know how you stand," he said.

"You can tell it to Diamond. When I lie down it'll be for good." He flicked his calloused thumb in the direction of the cutdown Greener, his eyes hard on John File. "And I'll not be by my lonesome."

"I will tell it to Diamond, since I'm like a old friend, Abel. But he isn't going to listen any more than me. I am telling you to stay out of it. But—you suit yourself."

"That is what I am aiming to do, mister."

When File had gone, Abel Tymes picked up the shotgun and checked its load. He didn't put it back in the gun cabinet, but stood it beside his chair on the far side of the desk, away from the door, where he could reach it easily.

That was where it was found a day later when the old Skandihoovian swamper from the Clean Whistle saloon came by with the marshal's lunch—as he did about every day—and discovered Marshal Abel Tymes lying dead on the floor with a bullet right through his forehead.

Al, the brindle cat, was seated by the body, seated in the pool of sunlight that came silently through the dirty window.

TWENTY-ONE

Abel Tymes was a widower, and there were not many mourners at the gravesite. Clint Adams had come. Clint had liked the stringy man with the knobby wrists and elbows. He was a type who wouldn't be long for the West, a type unique in the country's history. An honest man, but a practical man; decent and at the same time human.

Clint knew, and he talked it over with Buzz, that Phoenix would be getting hold of another deputy marshal to replace Abel Tymes. And too, they would be sending someone to investigate the killing.

"I don't think it was a very smart thing to do," Buzz observed to Clint. "I mean, seeing that it likely was Diamond's play."

"Abel might have pushed them too far," Clint suggested. "Maybe something like that. I agree with you. I doubt a man as smart as Cole Diamond would have done such a thing. It had to be someone acting on their own."

"Are you thinking John File?"

"It could be. You know, Tymes was a man who didn't let anyone backwater him. It could be File." Then he said softly, "Abel Tymes was a man, one of the last of a breed."

He was reflecting on this, more and more sure that there must have been something personal about the killing, as he stood with head bared at the slender service offered at the Kilton Wells cemetery the following day.

Few attended, mostly a few old ladies who attended all the town's funerals, a couple of curiosity people, two small boys from who knew where, the old swamper who had discovered the body and had liked Abel Tymes, and who now appropriated Al, his cat. And Clint Adams. A dozen people, give or take.

It was at the end, as everyone was leaving, that he saw her. At first he hadn't recognized her, but as the crowd began to break up he saw she was looking at him. It was the tall blonde with the hazel eyes who had been thrown from her horse and whose animal he had caught for her. And she was coming toward him.

"Hello, Mr. Adams. I don't know if you remember me. I'm Melissa Foster. You were kind enough to help me recently when my horse threw me."

"I certainly do remember you, Miss Foster. Good to see you again with no after effects from your spill, I trust."

They were walking side by side away from the dispersing group of mourners and soon they were quite alone, walking down the hill to the town.

"I take it you were a friend of Abel Tymes," he said conversationally and keeping his walk slow so that there would be more time to open the relationship. He found her very attractive, even more so than when she was lying on the ground after being thrown from her horse. Her hazel eyes were set wide beneath a high forehead, and though she was tall for a girl, she was not as tall as he. He could tell instinctively that she must have a delightfully proportioned body.

"Marshall Tymes was actually a friend of my father," she said. "An old friend as a matter of fact."

"Then it's nice that you could attend the funeral. I gather that Abel didn't leave any family."

"His wife died some years ago, and I believe he had a son and daughter, but they're in California or someplace like that."

He liked her quiet, rather brisk English accent.

"Are you English, I take it?" Clint asked.

"No. I was born in Wyoming, and my dad brought me here when I was quite young. I—I went to school in England."

"I see."

They had reached the main part of town and he didn't want to let her go. There was something in her manner too that seemed hesitant.

"May I say, Miss Foster, that you seem to have something on your mind. I hope I'm not intruding, but then— Look, how about joining me for a little something. It's noon now, and there's a restaurant right over there."

She looked at him for a moment, stopping right where she was, as though considering something. "All right, that would be nice."

The restaurant was a small place and not very full of people. They found a table in the corner and sat opposite each other.

For a few moments they discussed the weather and one or two other general subjects. But Clint could see that she still had something on her mind. He was about to speak about it again when she suddenly came out with it.

"I—you're wondering, Mr. Adams . . ."

"Please call me Clint."

"Clint," Her smile was sweet and more open than it had been.

She was secretive, he decided, but a little shy.

"Please call me Melissa," she said.

He smiled at her warmly, feeling something begin to stir in him, and open. He looked down at her hands, which were lying on the table near her plate. They were well shaped, soft, yet not weak looking at all.

"I—I owe you an apology," she said. "A rather big apology."

He couldn't help but show his surprise. "Might I ask what for, Melissa?"

He detected a trace of color in her cheeks which, he found to be charming, as she went on. The more he looked at her the more he decided she was truly beautiful.

"I—you see, my father was—his name was Tolliver. Clay Tolliver. Clayton," she added, holding his eyes with hers.

"Tolliver? You mean . . ."

"The . . . he was shot when you were with him. At the livery. You remember . . ."

"Of course I remember. I remember him very well. But you said your name was . . ."

"He wasn't my real father. I don't know who my parents were. I am, was an orphan, but I won't go into the details. Clay and Mary Tolliver took me in. Mary died when I was quite young. And Clay took on my education. He was not a poor man. Not by any means. But he got laid off by the railroad and he got sick and came down here for his health, his lungs. It was very hard for him. Then, just a short while ago, the railroad offered him a job back. And that picked him up. He'd been doing anything he could to make ends meet. As you saw, he was a hostler. He'd lost his money, though he'd scraped to send me to the best schools he could. He really . . . I owe him everything."

Clint saw the tears standing in her eyes And he wanted to reach out and touch her, comfort her. But she took a grip on herself and, lifting her head high, she resumed.

"I—I made a terrible fool of myself and I want to apologize."

"Do you mean you blamed me for your father's getting shot and killed?"

"Yes, yes I did."

"Well, it was my fault in a way. Whoever did that shooting was trying to hit me. And they unfortunately killed your dad."

"I went sort of crazy when I heard it. I—I wanted to kill you. And . . ."

"And I'm glad you missed," Clint said, filling in. "You came close."

Her mouth dropped and she stared at him. "You mean to say you knew it was me shooting at you out there in Big Tom Valley?"

"No, I didn't. I just put it together now."

"I . . . I don't know what to say . . ."

"Don't say anything, Melissa. You've said it all."

Her hazel eyes were enormous as she looked directly at him. "You mean you're not angry?"

"I'm relieved that you missed. But of course you luckily don't know much about shooting."

He saw his remark strike her as she flushed again. "Well, actually, I'm considered an excellent shot. I believe I wanted to miss. I've never shot anyone. As I said, I went a bit crazy. And I think something—I know something in me didn't want to."

"Maybe that's why you shot into the sun," Clint said simply, and he smiled fondly at her. Reaching out, he touched her hand as he watched the tears of relief come into her eyes.

For a moment she let him hold her hand, then she turned hers so that their palms were together. Clint immediately felt his passion surging through him.

"I'd better go now," she said, withdrawing her fingers from his.

"I want to see you again, Melissa."

"I know."

"Soon."

"I need a little time, Clint."

"Of course. I understand. I'm not impatient."

This brought a smile to her face. "Oh yes you are."

And as he stood up he wondered how in fact he was going to wait. She was adorable.

They parted outside the restaurant and then Clint walked down to the livery, saddled Duke, and rode out of town. It was clear that the killing of Abel Tymes indicated the final act in the drama of the homesteaders versus Cole Diamond and the stockgrowers. He was pretty sure Diamond wouldn't have ordered the killing, and so the likely suspect in his mind had to be John File. Tymes, being an ornery type when the mood took him, could have crossed File. Or maybe they'd known each other in the past. Clint knew all about John File, and Abel Tymes had told him he'd been in that line of work himself, that is, he'd packed a gun and had known how to use it. Maybe an old feud?

He decided it didn't matter. The deed was done. Tymes was dead and it was going to trigger a few things. He would bet Diamond was hopping mad about it. Somebody upsetting the applecart like that and opening the door for a federal marshal to come in.

He rode quickly back to Buzz's homestead, through the late afternoon with its dying light sounding through the land and, as it always did at that hour, calling something special in him. He wished he wasn't mixed up in it. He wished he was just riding out to spend the night with his friends Buzz and Wendy, a quiet evening watching the sunset and maybe swapping a story or two.

And but for the fact that there was Abel Tymes' killing hanging over them, and the imminence of a small cattle war, it was a fine evening. The three of them discussed the situation in detail, but then they took time to enjoy each other's company too.

Clint found the evening especially to his taste when not very long after he had lain down on his bunk he heard the footsteps and in she came.

He was already naked under the bedclothes, and she instantly dropped her clothes after locking the door. He thought for an instant of Melissa Foster, but she faded quickly from his mind as the soft and willing Wendy wound her arms and legs around him and he mounted her.

TWENTY-TWO

Buzz had ridden around to his neighbors, the other homesteaders, and again argued the need for them to get together to fight the Association. It was a last-ditch try, and it got nowhere. In vain he pointed out to them that with the big cattlemen running the gather without their participation to cut out their own slicks and brand them, they would end up with a good deal less than damn little.

But they were few, and they had been successfully divided by Diamond through fear, avarice, and the false hope that things would work out, that the picture wasn't as black as Buzz Fahnstock was painting. Even his outrage over the murder of Abel Tymes failed to move them.

Buzz was furious.

"I can't figure such ornery, scared-of-their-own-shadows men. Hell—they ain't men. They don't see they'll be closed out, picked off. If not killed into the bargain." He complained loudly and at length to Clint and Wendy.

"There's nothing you can do," Clint pointed out. "Except be reasonable. People are the way they are. Stop expecting things from them, especially more than they're able to give."

"But they're having their land stole from right in front of their eyes! They're blind! And they're just folding up and moving out."

"They've got children, families," Clint pointed out. "You'd feel different if you had kids about." And he was sorry he'd said it, thinking of Buzz's wife and how they had wanted children; and then she'd died. But it was said. He watched his friend's face fall a little, and his conviction seemed to stumble.

Then he seemed to rouse himself. "You're telling me I ought to pack up and leave too, Clint? Is that it?"

"Buzz, slow down, man. I am not telling you anything of the kind. I'm only suggesting that you take it slow. We need to think it through a little better."

"But I've told them Diamond stole Cantwell's homestead from right under his nose. And from under theirs too. Anybody with half a brain has got to know that Diamond either killed Cantwell himself or ordered it. And I know and by God so do you that that damn quitclaim deed was forged. Tymes knew that. I just know he knew it!"

"And Tymes is dead," Clint pointed out. "I'm also sure he knew it. I also would put my money on that paper being a forgery. But none of us can prove it."

Buzz was by now nearly beyond words. Wendy entreated him to sit down, to rest, to lie down on his bed before he worked himself into a severe coughing attack. He had already started to wheeze.

"Clint, isn't there something we can do to get this bull-headed man to lie down and rest and not kill himself?" And she turned back to Buzz. "Don't you see if you get sick and drop dead that you'll be helping Cole Diamond!"

This got through to him. He sat down, he wiped his forehead with his shirt-sleeve. He released an enormous sigh, shaking his head slowly.

Leaning forward with his forearms on his knees he let his hands hang down between his legs. His words addressed the floor. "I know. You're both right. I just wish there was something I could do. We could do." He looked up. "Is it still *We*, Clint."

"You bet your britches," said the Gunsmith.

"And you can bet your shirt too," Wendy added.

"I appreciate it," Buzz said softly. And both of them heard the sincerity in his voice. "But what can we do? Nothing? Just sit here?" And then he added, "Clint, I got you into this, and I want you to know how I feel about all the help and support you've given me so far. But I can't ask any more of you."

"That's right you can't." Clint answered him with a grin. "So from now on I'm just going to do what I want, which is to do what I can to get these people out of the valley. Or at least to get them to leave you and Wendy alone."

He was standing in the middle of the room and all at once both Buzz and Wendy took a second look at him. It was clear that Clint Adams had come to some sort of decision.

"What you got, Clint?" Buzz asked.

"I've got a prayer and a hope, and I've got myself," the Gunsmith said. "The thing is to hit someone where he's the weakest. Right?"

"Right," Buzz agreed. "But where is Diamond weak? Or any of the others in the Association? Hell, man, Diamond has got the money, the guns; he's got John File and they'll all be siding him if and when you and he go up against each other. Clint, they'll cut you down. They don't face a man fair."

"That is what I know," Clint agreed. "But every man has his weakness." And he was suddenly remembering the target site and what he had felt there when he'd looked at the targets. And he remembered something, some rumor he'd heard about John File some years ago. A hunch? A bluff? The only way to enter the game now was boldly. He grinned at his two friends. "Like you say, Buzz, they've got all the cards."

"All the aces," Buzz said.

"But the joker is wild," Clint put in. "And we've got the joker."

"Joker?" said Wendy. "Who has the joker?"

"That's us," Clint said. "And the joker is wild." He walked to the door of the room and then turned with his hat on the back of his head. "I was just thinking of something. Every man has his weakness, but so does every woman. Jealousy, my friends. Jealousy is the joker."

He left them both with puzzlement written all over their faces. But it was not the time to tell what at this point he was only half-guessing. But there were those two targets, and there was the determined young woman who was bent on being the "best"—whatever that meant. A woman who—it was obvious—would go all the way to achieve her goal.

Within minutes he had saddled Duke and was on his way to the gather of the cattle herd.

In the early afternoon, with the hot sun beating down

on him he sat his horse looking down from a promontory at the cattle gathering below. He had taken pains to be well covered from any inquisitive outriders, and he had a good view. Especially visible were Diamond's gunmen ringing the herd in case any homesteaders tried to interfere.

It looked like a full complement of cowhands were there to cut out the new calves and brand them. Clint enjoyed watching the scene below. It had been a while since he had done any roping and branding, but he appreciated fully the action.

Taking out his field glasses he studied the cowhands at work more closely. The roper really knew what he was doing. For Clint it was pure pleasure to watch the way the man rode his pinto horse right into the gather, having first built his loop with easy care. Then with one, maybe two turns of his arm he laid the wide loop onto the calf which had been hazed out of the bunch by other cowhands, and let that little terrified animal walk right through the loop till he reached his hind legs. With a dazzling pull the roper then drew up on the noose so that one hind leg of the calf was caught. The animal stumbled, crying out with fear and anger.

Meanwhile, two men on foot came in fast, one grabbing the calf at its haunch and at the foreleg and shoulder and with a great heave dumping the animal on its side, the other bending the foreleg and kneeling on the calf's neck to hold him down while the first man spread the animal's hind legs. A third man now approached to castrate the animal, making it a steer, while a fourth brought the branding iron which had been heating in the fire and burned the brand into the animal's rump. The final step was to notch one ear for quick recognition; and then the appalled animal was released to go bawling for its mother wherever she might be in the great mass of struggling, bellowing beef.

The noise, the smell of burned hair and flesh, the bawling of the calves trying to mother-up, and the cows bellowing for their calves filled the sky.

The men worked like dancers with a rhythm wholly appropriate to the work at hand. Clint found it always beautiful to watch and this time was no exception. Nor was he concerned for the moment over the fact that the calves were not necessarily the legal or moral property of the owner of their new brand. He was delighted simply to watch the men at their work. Here he saw a true comradeship having nothing to do with property, guns, money, tempers, and reputation.

And again he watched the man on horseback carefully, expertly building his loop, walking his pinto pony into the herd, selecting the right calf and then easy-as-you-please snagging that little animal and then, with his cowpony trained to the slightest nuance of movement, dragging the calf out to the calf-busters and brander and castrator.

He didn't know how long he'd been there—but judged it to be a good twenty minutes—when he saw her. She came riding in with Cole Diamond, and while Cole walked his big sorrel around the herd talking to various men, she continued to sit her dappled gray watching the action.

Through the field glasses Clint studied her. She was sitting erect on her pony, almost stiff, and he could appreciate the contours of her bust, and even the line of her smooth jaw. She seemed wholly consumed with the excitement of the moment. Yes, she was thrilled; he could see that. The noise, the smell, the sweating men; and he saw how now and again someone or other stole a glance her way. She was rather like a queen reviewing the troops, he decided. But a queen who was perhaps interested in more than the surface.

Every now and again he had stopped looking and taken a moment or so to check around him that he had not been spotted. And he did so now. He saw nothing, yet he felt a sense of something not the same. Without a second's hesitation he knew it was time to leave. Indeed he saw that Cole Diamond had the same idea, for he'd just ridden up to the girl and now together they were starting off into a fast canter, evidently heading toward town.

As he walked Duke back down the thin trail he felt his unease growing stronger. Yes, there was someone who had cut his trail. He decided on a surprise tactic and booted Duke into a gallop.

For a good distance they rode hard down the trail until he found a place that would be suitable. They had rounded a low cutbank and swept up a slight elevation toward a thick stand of mesquite and paloverde. He knew his pursuers were two and not far behind, for he hadn't pushed Duke to the limit, he wanted to trap them. Dismounting quickly he led the horse into the trees and, finding an almost illegible trail, followed it up to the top of the cutbank where he was hidden from the trail below which he'd just left. They had circled back in such a way that Clint was now above the trail and had a clear view of whoever would be riding along it.

He pulled the Winchester out of its scabbard and waited behind a big rock. In only a few moments he heard the horses. They were coming on fast, obviously two of Diamond's "regulators."

He could easily have killed them both. But the war

had not yet broken out into the open, and he didn't want to be the starter. Cole Diamond needed only something like that to justify his own actions.

So he fired a shot at the feet of the lead horse, almost spooking the animal right out of the trail and all but dumping its rider. Both men pulled up fast, sawing like mad on their reins and one even grabbing leather.

"Throw up your hands!" Clint moved right after he spoke in order to confuse them on his whereabouts. And when the second man was slow in raising his hands he fired another round.

"I said—up!"

This time there was no hesitation. But both were having trouble with their horses and each lowered a hand to control his mount.

"All right, you can bring them down. Drop your guns, into that bush. But one funny move and you are done for. Now turn those animals around and cut back fast to where you were. Right now!"

He watched severely while they turned their horses. They didn't hesitate. He could tell they wouldn't take a chance. They likely knew who he was and they wanted survival. He waited till the sound of the drumming hooves had died. Then he led Duke back down the trail and mounted him and galloped on toward Kilton Wells.

TWENTY-THREE

At the Double D main house Cole Diamond and his fellow stockmen sat around a table while a Mexican manservant cleared away the dishes. In a moment a second Mexican appeared with glasses and a bottle of brandy. The guests and their host had eaten well, and now they let their conversation subside as the brandy was poured and Cole offered cigars.

"It's all shipped all they way from Frisco," Cole said proudly, referring to both brandy and cigars. "I hope you men appreciate it."

"Ah, we do, Cole, we do!" said Lije Millerby, following with a chuckle of appreciation. "And the meal too, let me add." Lije raised his glass and all followed suit except Cole who waited. "To our host," Lije said. "Your health, Cole."

Cole Diamond inclined his head in appreciation. And then himself took a drink, silently toasting the health of his guests with a gesture of his raised glass.

Now the men sat back enjoying their cigars, their brandy, and their thoughts too. Things were clearly going well, as planned.

"Perhaps," Cole said, leaning forward with one elbow on the table, while his hand held his brandy glass. "Perhaps you'd like to know that McAdoo has agreed to sell. It means we won't have to worry about going through the Quinn place."

All voiced approval at that, and Harry Grim beamed, as they settled back again into their seats. It was a good moment, the moment of first victory. The roundup had gone off without a hitch. They'd caught plenty of slicks, and Jay Whiting, Cole Diamond's cattle foreman, would have the count in the morning. But they could all tell it was going to be high; a whole new herd branded with their five irons. They had all worked hard together as the Association. Clever! Especially clever, Cole was thinking, since it was Jay Whiting, his trusted foreman, doing the count. And if there were any slicks left by chance, Jay knew which brand to use.

"They'll fight back," he was saying now. "Of course, I—we have been playing it easy to keep within the law. We all respect the law and so we don't wish any unlawful acts. And I think it's a hell of a shame about Abel Tymes." He paused briefly while a murmur went around the table. "What I am saying is, let the squatters strike first. We've got plenty of time to wait. We've got the beef branded and we can wait. There's not all that much hurry to get them up onto Blue Mountain for the summer feed. They're likely still mothering up."

"But Cole," said George Macklin. "That'll give them the advantage. We all know the best defense is a strong offense, and if we wait they'll jump something sure as shootin'!"

"No." Cole was shaking his big head. "Our patience will put us right with the law. Let them do something, start something; we'll be like lambs waiting for the slaughter, except, let me assure you, gentlemen, it will be them that get slaughtered!"

"Right enough," Wes Monigan put in. "I'm with that."

Harry Grim mumbled something, but Cole and the others took it to be agreement. And even Macklin was nodding.

"So all we've got to do now is get past Fahnstock's place," said Lije Millerby. "Exceptin' he sure as hell hasn't been in any mind to sell."

"And what about Phoenix sending a new marshal?" Harry Grim asked. "The next one might be worse than Tymes."

"We won't get a man for several weeks, even a couple of months," Cole said. "That's the first thing I found out about after the shooting. I have friends in Phoenix."

"But, Cole, Fahnstock, especially with Adams siding with him, is a stone wall," Wes Monigan was saying.

Cole Diamond waited while all heads turned to see what he would say in response to this statement.

"All I can say is that I think we can get our cows up onto Blue Mountain."

"But how?"

Cole Diamond leaned back in his chair with his arms stretched forward and his hands flat on the table. "By finding a way to remove the obstacle."

"A legal way, Cole?" Monigan asked.

"A—uh—way, Wes." And the smile stayed at Cole Diamond's lips.

Lije Millerby cleared his throat loudly. "You've got something, have you, Cole?"

"Gentlemen, excuse me if I seem—well, not too forward at the moment. I'm working on it. And I want to be sure it's going to work before I spell it out. Will you bide with me?" His tone couldn't have been more open and frank and the group as a man agreed to bide with him. Why not? Cole had run it this far, and was doing a good job.

In only a few moments more they finished their brandy and cigars and broke up.

Cole walked them to the door and saw them out. Then, relighting his cigar, he walked back to the table, sat down, and poured himself another brandy. He was still sitting there, going over his plan when the door opened and the "love of his life" walked in.

She had changed from her riding habit and she was looking ravishing. Cole said so.

"I'm feel ravish— How do you say this?" Carla said.

"Ravish," Cole said, pouring her a brandy, "means to—uh—enjoy the pleasure of the flesh, my dear."

"Pleasure. Is that all you think of, Cole?"

"Don't you, my dear?" He handed her the glass of brandy, smiling, his eyes dropping to her partly exposed bosom where the beginning of her cleavage could be seen.

Her laughter tinkled as she sipped her brandy and let her eyes fall to his crotch. "You have not forgotten about Fill?"

"File," he corrected.

"I know it is File."

"Except when you put on your Spanish accent, eh, my dear?" Cole was chuckling, hugely confident with the way he was running the Stockmen's Association and with the vision of soon controlling Big Tom Valley once he was rid of Fahnstock.

"Be careful," she said, her voice suddenly hard. "I am what I am, and you are what you are. Don't try getting nasty with me, Cole. We each one has his or her role."

His smile was suddenly stuck on his face as he realized to his dismay that she had once again bested him. At such moments he always found it necessary to remember that much as he adored her sexuality, her charm, even up to a point her teasing, that the lovely lady could have her uses. It was essential that he, Cole Diamond, come out of this passage-at-arms with the squatters with lily-white hands. Good old Cole. That was the thing, his role. The mediator, the genial lord of Big Tom Valley. But Cole also knew how careful he had to be. The only thing that could undo him was his damn jealousy. His great weakness. And according to the reports he'd been receiving he had plenty to be jealous about.

"Hows ever," Carla was saying, "I be tired, my little Cole, darling. Could we not cuttle a liddle?"

He chuckled, she had changed her mood completely. He loved it. He adored it, relished it, savored, worshiped it as she undid his pants and with both hands eagerly yanked out his bone-hard penis and, lifting her skirt, sat down on it taking it deep into her.

Afterwards they slept, right there on the floor on the bearskin rug.

TWENTY-FOUR

Nothing was more clear to the Gunsmith than the fact that the cattle trouble in Big Tom Valley would not be settled without his direct confrontation with John File. File had been brought in for that very purpose, and the more Clint thought about that fact, the more he knew that the sooner he stopped File the more chance there would be of stopping Cole Diamond.

He had ridden into Kilton Wells with the express purpose of finding Melissa Foster. There was something that had kept pulling at him—some thought, a feeling—since his meeting with her; and it would not leave him alone. it kept nagging at him, and finally he'd found his question.

She had told him where she lived in town and his hopes were answered when he found her at home. She was surprised to see him and asked him in for a cup of coffee.

"I wanted to ask you about something that you mentioned in our last conversation, Melissa," he said as they sat in the little parlor of the clean, neat little house.

"What was that?" She gave a little smile to encourage him, and, even though his question was important, he had a moment to feel his breath catch at her loveliness.

"You said something about your father working for the railroad, I believe."

"Yes, Dad worked in the office in Cheyenne. Then, as I said, he lost his job, was laid off. That was very hard on him, but . . . Why do you ask?"

"Didn't you say something to the effect that they were thinking of hiring him back?"

"Well, actually, now that you mention it, I'm not sure it was the same railroad. You see, Dad always just referred to 'The Railroad,' and when he mentioned that he was going to get a job with the railroad again we just got all excited about it, and I don't know whether it might not have been another company or whatever they're called."

"But where, where was he going to have this job? I'm sorry to keep questioning you so, but it's very important."

"Why, right here, I'm sure." She looked surprised at his question.

"But there isn't any railroad here."

"Dad said they were thinking of building a line here. For the cattle, I believe."

It came to him then like a lightning bolt why he had felt Diamond was holding something up his sleeve, was hiding something, as he'd put it to Buzz. The railroad. But of course that was why he wanted Big Tom Valley. A spur would have to come through there. And as far as

Cole Diamond was concerned, the homesteaders were right in his way to own the land and sell it to the railroad at a huge profit.

Clint had a grin on his face as he looked at the girl now.

"You look like the cat that swallowed the canary," she said, smiling at him fondly.

"I'm smiling because I've finally dug out what has been picking at me for some time. Why there was such a ruckus going on about the homesteads in Big Tom Valley; all under the pretense, of course, that the big stockgrowers want to preserve their short route to Blue Mountain when they move their herds up there for the summer feed."

"But that wasn't why Dad was shot, is it?"

He shook his head. "No, they were after me." He watched her handle that again and admired how she did so.

Reaching out, he touched her hand, and she held his fingers.

"I have to go now," he said.

"I know. I see that you need to go, and do whatever you have to do."

"I'll be back."

"I hope so," Melissa said.

And without another word he stood up, walked to the door, and was gone.

Fifteen minutes later he was up on Duke riding out to Buzz Fahnstock's TeaKettle ranch. He was leading a hired pack horse loaded with two heavy cowhide panniers.

It ws late when he reached his destination—to be confronted by a furious Buzz.

"Clint, you want to know who killed Abel Tymes?"

Clint had just walked in the door when Buzz fired the question at him. Out of the side of his eye he saw Wendy watching.

"Buzz . . ." But he paid no attention to her. He was enraged.

"Who?" said Clint. "And what are you so mad about? Was it File?"

"No! It was not John File! It was Buzz Fahnstock!"

Clint looked at his friend impassively. "So that's what the word is in the valley, eh?"

"You haven't heard that in town?"

"I only made a couple of stops, and they weren't at the saloons where I reckon I would have heard such a thing."

"Well, that's the word, let out by that son of a bitch Diamond. And I am going to beat the living shit out of him! Claims Tymes found out I stole Cantwell's money so I shot him!"

It was clear to Clint that his friend had been drinking. At this point Wendy tried again to remonstrate with him.

"Buzz, lie down for a while and calm down, will you."

But Buzz was also furious at the news of Noah McAdoo selling out to the stockmen at the last minute. He was also enraged at the early gather, and he'd heard about Diamond running some of his own herd in with the Association stuff.

"And I hear Diamond's been slapping his own brand on what he should be branding for the Association," he went on, his face red and perspiring.

"I saw some of the Double D on those slicks when I was out there," Clint said. "But that doesn't matter."

"What do you mean, it doesn't matter!"

"What matters, my friend, is that those cattle are

going to come through here like a tornado—right through the middle of your spread. Unless we stop them."

"I know that. I know that! Clint, let it be known that I am ready! Buzz Fahnstock is ready! I don't care if they have got a dozen John Files and fifty Cole Diamonds, I am ready!" He lifted his glass of whiskey, which had been beside him on the table, and started clomping around the room still in a fury. Then suddenly he stopped and sat down abruptly and without warning. It was as though he had just collapsed from his great exertions. Luckily there was a chair under him. Even so he almost fell out of it.

Wendy rushed to his side. "Buzz, you're drunk and we are putting you to bed."

He didn't argue. He had a smile on his face now, and he let them help him into the bedroom where he flopped right onto his back on the bed and was snoring almost before he hit.

TWENTY-FIVE

Clint awakened two or three times during the night, with his thoughts on the plan he had been making. And finding the girl beside him. She appeared to be sleeping peacefully after their lovemaking, and he didn't rouse her. He remained quite still, thinking over his plan. First, the confrontation with the cattle if they should start earlier than anticipated by Wendy and Buzz. And second, the question of John File. For the real fight, he knew, was with the tall man. He lay absolutely still, simply allowing his thoughts to flow through him. And then all of a sudden he knew what it was that had been bothering him about the targets. The drawings were File. There was no mistaking now the bend of the head and the hawklike nose. And Clint recollected the stories he'd heard about File's girl. No question but that it was Carla Onterra, if indeed that was her real name, though it surely didn't matter. And suddenly the realization that he had been sleeping with File's ex-girl hit him. Not that he cared. But he wondered about Carla. He had heard stories of how the man had humiliated her. Although he didn't know the details he could imagine what it would have done to someone like Carla. Surely that was why she was so possessed with firearms. And now he wasn't sure whether she was gunning for himself or File. Or—both?

In the morning he was up early; before dawn. He unloaded his supplies from the panniers and carefully checked everything. Hearing a step he looked up to find Wendy approaching.

"Dynamite?" she said, raising her eyebrows.

"Beats guns by a country mile when used in a certain way."

"Like how?" said Buzz's voice as he came through the door of the shed where Clint was checking his purchase.

"Like stopping a herd of cattle from stampeding your spread."

"Where you figure's the best place, Clint?"

"Jack Crossing. There's a cutbank on one side where they'll be fording the creek, and almost exactly opposite some high rocks."

"Sounds right to me," Buzz said. And he grinned. "I got me a head like a hoss this morning."

"I'll get some coffee," Wendy said.

When they were seated in the kitchen of the stone house Clint outlined his plan.

"They'll for sure come through that section where McAdoo put up his barbed wire."

"I'll bet on it," Buzz agreed. "But that's a way from the creek. The crossing actually is on McAdoo's property."

"I know," Clint said.

Buzz studied it a moment. "Are you meaning what I'm thinking you're meaning, Clint?"

"You know that's the only place to set something up. The rest is open country."

"But it's on McAdoo's land," Wendy said. "Does that make a difference?"

"It means they'll maybe be caught in surprise," Clint said. "And anyway, it's Diamond's land now. So we're simply carrying the war to him. If we wait till his riders get here with the herd we won't have a chance."

"I'm for it," Buzz said, slapping his hand down on the table. "Now the thing is to find out when they're planning to move the herd."

At this point Clint told them about his conversation with Melissa Foster and about Clay Tolliver and the railroad.

"By jiminy," Buzz said. "By God, that explains a helluva lot of it. You were right about something more that we weren't seeing, Clint. Diamond is double-crossing his partners to boot!"

"He's selling his partners out, is what you're saying, Buzz." And Wendy looked at him quizzically.

"That's what is happening, Wendy."

"But there's something I don't understand. How is he selling the others out? I feel he is, but I don't see just what he's doing."

"The spur will have to go through Big Tom Valley," Clint explained. "As I understand it," and he glanced at Buzz for agreement, "there's been the rumor of a spur and cattle shipping point for some time. And recently it's died down. Probably the dying down has been helped along by Diamond. All he's got to do now is name his price when the railroad wants to come in."

"And when he sells his land to the railroad, his partners in the Stockmen's Association will lose their route to Blue Mountain for their herds." Wendy was nodding her head as she spelled it out to herself.

"Any value in our telling Millerby and his friends what Diamond's doing?" Buzz asked, looking at Clint and then at Wendy.

"He'll just deny it. He can always promise he won't sell if he's pushed to the wall. There's nothing they can do anyway. It's his land." Clint took a drink of his coffee.

"Seems then the first thing is to set up for Diamond and all those beeves," Buzz said. "When do you figure is a likely time?"

Clint was already on his feet. "Right now." He had walked to the window in the front room while they watched him through the door leading in from the kitchen.

"You see something?" Buzz called, getting to his feet.

"I see my invitation is about to arrive."

When Buzz joined him at the window they both stood there watching the rider approaching down the long draw that led to the ranch.

"Looks like that woman," Buzz said.

"That's who it is." He turned back into the room. "Buzz, I think they'll try to pull two things at once— one, to get me away from here, and the second while I'm away to run their herd through."

"The buggers. I'd better get onto checking their herd. I reckon they're holding them in Butte Basin, just east."

Wendy had joined them at the window now, and Clint had turned back to watch the approaching rider. Without taking his eyes away he said, "You can help

Buzz pack those panniers down to Jack Crossing and cache them in a dry place."

"But what about the cattle?" Buzz asked. "We need to keep an eye on when they'll start moving them."

"How about sending Clancy?" said Clint. "Can you trust him?"

"I have so far," Buzz said, and cut his eye to Wendy, who nodded in agreement "Clancy Calhoun one time told Diamond's foreman, Jay Whiting, to go piss up a rope."

Clint grinned, still not taking his eyes off the approaching rider. "Good enough. I reckon he is one of us."

Buzz laid his hand on his friend's arm. "Clint, be careful."

He turned from the window then and grinned at Buzz Fahnstock. "I will," he said. And with a quiet smile for Wendy he quickly checked his sidearm, reset his hat on his head, and walked out to meet Carla Onterra who was just pulling up on her big dappled gray horse. In the distance he again spotted the two horsemen covering her.

TWENTY-SIX

He liked the way she was just slightly breathless as she rode up. He could see that she had been pushing the big gray, for there was sweat starting on its flanks and he was still restless from the ride, jabbing his head about while the bridle clinked and there was the soft squeak of leather as the girl shifted her weight in her saddle.

"We meet again, Clint."

"It's my pleasure, Carla. What can I do for you?"

"I carry a message."

"From John File."

Her surprise was quick, but she smiled then to try to cover it. "You are good at guessing."

"What does he want?"

"He wants to talk with you."

"Fine. But you can tell him it's just as far from me to him as it is from him to me. I'll be looking forward to seeing him." He looked up at the sun, then took a quick look in the direction of the two riders who were waiting for her some distance away. "You got anything else?"

She leaned down from her saddle then. "I want to see you, Clint."

"Don't you think that would make your boyfriend jealous?"

"Cole? He is jealous of everyone and everything."

"No—John File."

He watched it hit her hard; he had not realized the extent of whatever she had been feeling for File all these years. He could see it went deep.

"I have nothing to do with him. I only give this message," she said, her voice cold. And then, her voice softer, "I not wish to, Clint. He maybe kill you."

"I'll be here if he wants to see me." And without anything further he turned and started back to the house. Her words came over his shoulder.

"But he say there—to meet him."

He heard the insistence in her voice, and realized he had judged correctly. They were trying to get him away from the ranch.

"Where does he want to meet?" he said, stopping and turning back to her.

"In the town. In Kilton Wells."

"I'll be there in the morning. Tell him." And he started walking to the house. Behind him he heard her say, "Adios, Clint, my friend." And then the big gray horse was drumming out of the yard toward the two riders who were waiting for her.

Buzz almost pounced on him as he walked in.

"So what's happening? We heard something about Kilton Wells. Is it File?" Buzz asked.

"Yes—File. But the thing is we know when they're

starting to move the herd," Clint said as he faced them in the middle of the room.

"Did she say something?" Wendy asked.

"Not like that. But they're trying to draw me off to town and that means they're ready to push the herd through."

Buzz turned to Wendy. "Will you tell Clancy to keep an eye on the herd? He can let us know when they start moving."

Clint was already at the door. "Let's get going. We don't have any time to waste. We've got to set up at Jack Crossing pretty damn quick."

They saddled their horses quickly and in a very short time they were on the trail to Jack Crossing. They were still within sight of the ranch when Wendy caught up with them.

Dusk was just starting to settle into the land when they reached the cutbank and the rocks on the other side of the creek. They had ridden carefully, watchful for any outriders who might be expecting unwanted visitors. It had slowed them, but all three were glad that they reached their destination without any untoward event.

"We'll be two on this side and one over here," Clint said. "That'll be me. And if Clancy shows up he can be with my side—here. So get your dynamite sticks out and hold your fire. They'll likely cross here in the morning. They'll expect a fight up at the ranch, not here I'll wager. So we have surprise on our side. But save on the dynamite; use your rifles when you can. Pick off the leaders. Drop them so the ones following stumble over them." He snapped out his commands because he felt darkness coming and he wanted his army of two to be sure of their layout well before dawn came.

They had just finished making their preparations when Clancy showed up. Clancy Calhoun was a man in his late fifties who looked like a piece of wood. He had a drooping mustache that reminded anyone who took stock of him of a Texas longhorn.

"They'll be moving 'em in the morning," Clancy said.

"How many men are they?" Clint asked.

"I'd reckon ten, a dozen—give or take. They ain't expecting big trouble—being as it's just yourselves, and I got real close and heard Diamond saying maybe you wouldn't even be there."

"He's here," Buzz said firmly, "and those bastards better know it!"

"We'll get some sleep," Clint said. "I'll take first watch, then Clancy will relieve me at midnight."

"And what about myself?" Buzz demanded. "I am not dead yet, by the Almighty!"

Clint had to grin at that. "You'll need everything you've got for tomorrow, and that is an order!"

Buzz looked at Wendy, who was glaring at him. Then he saw the sense of it. "You got me surrounded," he said and let out a huge sigh.

Presently they settled down and Clint, feeling wide awake, kept his vigil. At midnight he was relieved by Clancy. He lay down on bare ground, but still didn't sleep. Or rather he half slept, for moments, still aware of anything that might be going on. The night passed uneventfully; the only thing that disturbed the quiet of the night and the night sounds of the animals was Buzz Fahnstock's snoring.

Clint was up before dawn, and riding Duke closer to the herd of cattle to investigate. As he approached he could hear them stirring, and now closer, the men calling to them and cracking the ends of their lariat ropes to get them moving.

He rode back to the others to report. Everyone was already up and Wendy had boiled coffee, which was most gratefully received. They drank it quickly and then manned their positions.

Shortly they began to hear the thundering reverberation of the cattle that were moving slowly toward the creek.

Each of the TeaKettle party had a supply of dynamite as well as rifle and cartridges and handguns. Each knew how to use their weapons. The plan was to turn and stampede the cattle, then while the Stockgrower men were trying to handle the stampede the TeaKettle men would fall back to a second position beyond the pass leading to Big Tom Valley. If their luck held they would repeat the operation. There were two other spots picked besides Jack Crossing, the final one being Buzz's homestead itself. Everything depended on timing, on whether their ammunition and dynamite were used carefully and effectively, and held out.

"We don't expect to stop them completely," Clint said, "but we're by God going to make it costly for them. Real costly. So that they'll know that not only this time, but any future time it will cost them dear."

He had just checked each of his three companions when they saw the leaders of the herd coming toward them. Clint had ordered everyone to hold their fire until he gave the signal.

He waited until the leaders were within easy reach, then, lifting his Winchester, fired at one of the front beeves. The animal dropped, and the others started to mill and then run as more shots rang out from Buzz and Wendy and Clancy. Meanwhile, the Stockgrower riders had pounded up, firing at where they thought the attack was coming from, but Clint had already ordered his companions to move away instantly from the site they'd fired from and take up a new position.

The riders came charging in, firing almost indiscriminately. There were plenty of them it seemed. Then, lighting a stick of dynamite, Clint sent it sailing right into the mass of the lead cattle. His companions immediately followed suit. Pandemonium instantly broke loose as the leaders reacted in terror. In moments the herd was out of control, stampeding beyond any possibility of holding them. The cowboys, and the gunmen too were racing their horses, trying to stem the great tide of terrified beef. But to no avail.

In the confusion, Clint and his three friends beat a swift retreat to their second redoubt, at the pass entering Big Tom Valley. Here they regrouped, and changed horses, which they had left there on their way down to the creek.

"I hate shooting good beef on the hoof," Buzz said. "But by heaven we turned 'em."

"Only for a while," Clint pointed out. "They're fighting mad now, and they'll be likely bringing up more guns."

His prediction proved right. It was nightfall by the time the herd was brought into a semblance of order and the men got them bedded down. The following morning they started them moving again.

It was now a full day past his appointment with John File in town, and he decided it would be at least still another day. The herd moved slower this time, the cowboys were more careful, the gunmen were out flanking closely, with spot riders going ahead to scout the land. Two came pretty close to where Clint and his companions were hidden but didn't spot them. They bedded down that night, expecting to move the herd the following morning after the beeves had rested.

"Think they're expecting another setup?" Buzz asked.

"They could be," said Clint. "So I think we'll take a chance and move down to those mesquite and paloverde trees. Some one of them might just take a notion that we'd try again. And that opening to the valley is too likely a spot. I mean, for anyone who's already suspicious."

"Good," Buzz said. "I like the way you improvise, Clint. It's the only way as far as I'm concerned."

"Let's just hope it works," Clint said, and he winked at Wendy, who was looking more adorable the more tired she got.

This time Clint gave the order to only throw the dynamite sticks, and not use rifles which more easily gave away their position. They located themselves and prepared themselves to wait.

It was halfway through the next forenoon when the herd came in sight. There were lead men ahead and they were heavily armed. Clint slipped swiftly around to his troops and assigned himself and Wendy to shoot at the lead riders, and Clancy and Buzz to throw the dynamite.

They waited. The sun bore down like fire but nobody moved. Each one had been warned about any metal that might catch the sun's rays and give away their position. So each had covered their weapons with cloth.

The cattle came closer, the lead men wary as they came through the opening into the valley, and they appeared to let down somewhat when they got the herd through without mishap. As they rode by the mesquite and paloverde trees Clint and Wendy had the two lead riders in their sights. They had ridden past and the herd was close now when he gave the signal to throw the dynamite. But the two riders were far ahead and almost out of sight by that time and so Clint realized they were risking an attack from their rear. Meanwhile, the dynamite sticks had struck into the lead cattle and created chaos. Clancy and Buzz threw more, from new positions. Clint dropped back, ordering Wendy to follow suit by waving his arm to indicate that they could be ready for the two lead riders when they came pounding back to the attack.

He had just dropped behind a rock when he saw the first one and shot him dead off his horse. The second had spotted Wendy and had fired, missing the girl but close enough to send a shower of wood as it glanced off one of the trees. Wendy fired back, heroically holding her ground. But it was Clint who brought the man down.

Meanwhile the herd was again stampeding and the men were riding hard, in all directions, it seemed, cursing at being hit again.

"Let's get out of here," shouted Clint. "They'll see it's useless to try to stop them and they'll come after us. In fact, they're doing that now!"

All four now booted their horses away from the scene, pounding hard and fast for the TeaKettle. None of them had seen any sign of Cole Diamond.

It was dusk when they reached the ranch, having gone a long way around to shake their pursuers. Finally, walking their tired horses, they came into the TeaKettle. All four were close to exhaustion, but Clint knew that the fight was only beginning.

TWENTY-SEVEN

It was the hottest part of the day, reaching toward high noon. He was thinking of Wild Bill as he rode into Kilton Wells. Wild Bill who had the speed and accuracy of a mountain lion. And the courage and tenacity. It was a day to think of Bill. This day that he was riding into town.

He had once again improvised on his plan, deciding to surprise File—and Diamond—by suddenly appearing. For File and Diamond, and Carla too would have figured that since he'd not come to town when he'd said he would that he was out at the cattle fight. And he wondered if Cole Diamond was in town or out with his men.

The main street was about deserted. As he rode past the Clean Whistle Saloon he spotted the old swamper, the Swede who'd discovered Abel Tymes' body, and had been his friend. The old man was sitting on a broken wooden chair with no back, leaning against the side of the Clean Whistle, chewing and now and again spitting. Al, the brindle cat, was lying prone on his side close by.

As the Gunsmith drew abreast, the old man kept right on chewing, not moving in his chair, but now imperceptibly nodding toward the north end of town, in the direction of the Double Eagle.

Clint didn't rein his horse, but as he walked him past the old Skandihoovian he said, just barely audibly, "Both of them?"

"File," the old man said, seeming not to interrupt his chewing as he said the words. "He just left, but he'll be back when he hears you're in town." And he closed one eyelid leaving the other eye wide open.

And Clint and Duke were past the old man who continued to sit there in the broken chair sunning himself and chewing and spitting without the slightest change of rhythm.

The only other life in the street was a dog with a piece off the end of his tail and a dour look on his face as Clint rode past. He drew rein at the Double Eagle and, stepping down, scanned the street once again. He had missed nothing on his way up, taking in the rooftops, the alleys, the shadow places. The town was half asleep, as towns are at noon, and yet there was a charge in the atmosphere. He could feel it, almost a crackling running through his body as he pushed open the batwing doors.

There were few customers, and most of them were in the darker parts of the room, nursing drinks at tables or simply sitting in the random chairs that lined the walls.

Nothing. The click of poker chips, and the more solid clonk of a billiard ball as it struck its target.

The bartender caught him the moment he entered, then started to cut a look toward the back room, but caught himself, yet not before the Gunsmith noticed the giveaway.

"I'll take a beer," Clint said as he stood up close to the bar, with his eyes in the mirror. He waited while the barkeep got the beer, his eyes watching the entire room through the mirror, which afforded him a view of the door toward which the bartender had unsuccessfully tried to retrieve his glance.

He didn't actually want anything to drink, but a glass of beer furnished his reason for being there. The drama of such moments always had their ritual, he noted again. At the same time you had to look out for surprises, death being the final ritual if you failed to do so.

No one had left the room. Clint had taken note of that. No message had been sent to any part out of the Double Eagle.

He had kept the little balcony in his mirror view at the same time, and, of course, the stairway leading up to it and its rooms. So far there had been no movement from up there. He was sure though that there must be at least some of the girls there, if not a customer or two. He had already noted that there was a stairway leading to the upstairs from the outside, and, in fact, had seen a man climbing up only a few days before when he'd chanced by. There was therefore the chance possibility that File could enter the building that way. But in the very moment that he was considering this, the door of the back room opened suddenly and Carla Onterra stepped out. She spotted him instantly, but gave no sign of recognition.

The Gunsmith had shifted his stance at the bar so that

he could make his draw without any interference or awkwardness on his part. He had three areas picked for his target. The batwing doors leading in from the street, the balcony which held the cribs for the girls, and the door of the back room. He could also throw down on anyone in the bar itself including the bartender.

Carla was walking toward the batwing doors when suddenly the Gunsmith had a hunch. In his mind's eye he saw the old swamper sitting in his chair outside the Clean Whistle. He had felt something at the time, but because of his feeling for Abel Tymes he hadn't taken full notice. But there had been something "extra" about the old man. He had somehow nodded his head in a strange way, as though he was trying to say something more than the words he was actually speaking. And, yes, he had winked; he had lowered one eyelid in that solemn wink. Why?

The Gunsmith had no more time to give thought to that for Carla was halfway across the room, halfway to the swinging doors; and just at that moment the batwing doors opened and a man entered. In the wink of an eye Clint Adams saw that it was one of the riders who had accompanied her each time to the TeaKettle. The man was already reaching for his gun when the Gunsmith shot him in the neck.

Carla hadn't made a move. She had stopped right in her tracks and stood watching the drama. When her eyes went toward the back room, the Gunsmith turned and shot the other gunman right between the eyes. The man had his gun halfway out of its holster. But Clint realized his clean shot had put him with his back to the balcony, though he was still half facing Carla.

"You are very fast, Mr. Gunsmith," she said. She

was wearing her buscadero with the brace of Colts. "Uh —please not to move. Stay still and I show you how fast is Carla Onterra."

When he saw her eyes flick, the Gunsmith understood how they had figured it out. His gun was back in its holster and he had fired two rounds.

"I have no intention of drawing on you, Carla."

"Why? Why not? Because I am a woman?"

"Because that's what I am saying, that's why. So cool off. Go play gunnie with someone else; with that fellow up on the balcony, behind me."

The room had frozen. At the first shooting a number of customers had hit the floor and they remained there. Others had been too paralyzed or too sensible to try moving out of their chairs.

Clint watched the wicked smile on Carla's face as her eyes went past him. And for a moment there was silence. Then Clint heard a door open on the balcony and a woman's voice saying something incoherent as her words were caught by the startling drama in the saloon below.

At the sound of the woman's voice Carla Onterra had gone white. "You bastard!" And her hand streaked to her hip. The gun was out and up—she was real fast, the Gunsmith had time to note—when the shot rang out from the balcony behind him and she dropped slowly to the floor.

Meanwhile, in that split moment, the Gunsmith had himself dropped to the floor, twisting as he went down and rolling and coming up with his Colt firing at the man on the balcony who already had his gun in his fist.

"Holy Mother of God . . ." muttered the all but paralyzed bartender as John File's bullet hit nowhere, while the Gunsmith drilled him right through the heart.

Clint Adams was up on his feet. "Where is Diamond?" he said to the bartender.

"He took off for his outfit when File and the girl came in."

"How long have they been here?" Clint was thinking of the old swamper who had lied to him but then had tried to tell him so.

"All day." The bartender was totally bald and his bare head was damp with sweat. Even his eyes appeared to be sweating. "They set it up for you."

"I reckon I figured that out," Clint said laconically.

"I mean I overheard them talking about it."

But Clint wasn't listening. He had knelt beside the dying girl.

"Gunsmith," she murmured. "You are like the light. Him never have a chance."

"Somebody get the doc," Clint said. "Lie easy," he said to her.

"I not want to live. I kill him if I could. I want to kill him when I see him with the woman up there. He . . . he was coming old. He ask me to help him. Challenge you and then he backshoot."

"Lie easy now."

"You move so fast, Gunsmith. But I am next fast." And she closed her eyes then.

Clint Adams was still kneeling beside her when the doc came.

"What happened?" he asked.

"A couple of people got shot," the Gunsmith said simply. And he stood up.

TWENTY-EIGHT

"There are some bodies out there," the Gunsmith said when he kicked in the door of the back room and walked in on Cole Diamond, who had just lighted a cigar. Clint's glance went instantly to the box of Searchlight matches and at the torn V on the cover. "So you were at the firing of Buzz Fahnstock's homestead."

"I had nothing to do with it, Adams, and that's the truth!" The big man wasn't looking so big now. He sat heavily in his chair, gazing somberly across at Clint Adams. The two men were alone in the room.

"I'll cut you in on any share you want, Adams. All I want is that you work for me. I've got a real big deal going. And it's going all the way."

"Your railroad deal isn't going anywhere," Clint said.

"You don't know, man!" Diamond half rose out of

his chair in protest. "You don't know what you're talk-ing about!"

"You're through, Diamond. You know it. You wouldn't be wanting me to work for you otherwise."

He had been standing just inside the room to the side of the doorway to protect his back when he heard the quick footsteps. Turning quickly, he was greeted by Buzz Fahnstock—disheveled, out of breath, flushed, but brilliantly happy.

"We beat 'em, Clint. They tried right up to the house to come through and we blew them the hell and gone out of there!" He looked hard at Diamond who had turned pale. "I see what happened outside. She was a damn good-looking woman."

"You killed her, Adams! Goddamn you!"

"No, Diamond. It was File. Her boyfriend."

Diamond was visibly shaken to his roots. "Her—what? What the hell are you saying!"

"I'm saying John File, her boyfriend of long, long standing."

Cole Diamond looked as though he'd been struck across the face with a pistol. He seemed to have lost all his blood. He rose from his chair, took a step, stag-gered. Then he managed to control himself. "My God . . . My God . . ." His words seemed to come on the last of his breath. He collapsed back into his chair.

"How's Wendy?" Clint asked.

"She's fine. I—Boy, she'd make a man a good wife."

"I agree. And I wish you both all the best."

"But I haven't even . . ." expostulated the reddening Buzz Fahnstock.

"But you will," said Clint with a big grin.

The moment allowed Cole Diamond to rally to his former self. He rose and stood before them. "I will still get you goddamn squatters out of Big Tom Valley, Fahnstock. I have the law on my side."

"That's what you might think, Diamond," Fahnstock snapped. "And the railroad. But I am taking that quit-claim deed to the federal marshal's office and having it checked for forgery. This here—" And he jerked his thumb over his shoulder to indicate the carnage in the bar outside, "and what's happened with the cattle will bring them running. They're not going to sit on their hands now."

By the time they went out to the bar again the room was back in order. Eyes followed the Gunsmith as he walked through with his friend Buzz Fahnstock; and tongues followed after.

"You coming on out?" Buzz said when they were outside.

"Later."

"Wendy'll be looking for you."

"Wendy is already looking for you, Mr. Fahnstock. I know the signs. Now skedaddle." And with a friendly hit on his friend's shoulder, he turned away and started toward the other end of town.

He would go out to the TeaKettle later to collect his warbag and other gear and his gunsmithy rig. And he'd have a drink with Buzz and Wendy.

But right now he had something else on his mind. He was mighty pleased to find her home. And he was even more pleased a short while later when he discovered the superb wonders of Melissa Foster's eager body. The Gunsmith wasn't a man to take credit to himself unduly, but in the present case he did feel he had earned it.

J. R. ROBERTS
THE GUNSMITH

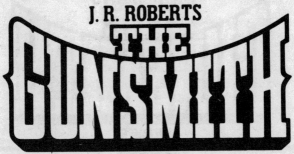

SERIES

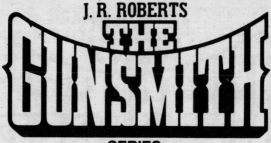

J. R. ROBERTS
THE GUNSMITH
SERIES